Catmagic

HOLLY WEBB

SCHOLASTIC INC.

New York Toronto London Auckland Sydney
Mexico City New Delhi Hong Kong Buenos Aires

ISBN-13: 978-0-545-12414-0
ISBN-10: 0-545-12414-X

All rights reserved. Published by Scholastic Inc., 557 Broadway, New York, NY 10012, by arrangement with Scholastic Ltd. SCHOLASTIC and associated logos are trademarks and/or registered trademarks of Scholastic Inc.

12 11 10 9 8 7 6 5 4 3 2 1   9 10 11 12 13 14/0

Printed in the U.S.A.
First U.S. edition, May 2009

For Jon, Tom, Robin, and William

1

I am not looking, I am not looking.

Lottie glared straight ahead, ignoring her mother, who was waving determinedly at her through the train window.

Lottie had hardly spoken to her since she'd broken the news two days ago. She was too angry — and if they discussed it, talked it all through, it would be real. Until just about now, Lottie had been convinced that somehow her mum's new job in Paris wasn't really going to happen, that if Lottie really hated the idea, her mum wouldn't go through with it. But it was getting too late to turn back now.

She wasn't going to see her mum all summer and they hadn't even properly said good-bye! Lottie turned suddenly, pressing her hand against the window.

Her mum wasn't there.

The train had already started, and all Lottie could see were strange faces gliding by. She turned right around in her seat, panicking. She didn't even know when she'd see Mum again! Peering frantically out of the corner of the window as the train curved out of the platform, she could see her mum's pink coat. She was still waving. Lottie waved back until the train was right out of the station. Then she sat down again, feeling shaky and sick, and very alone.

A crackly voice over the speaker announced the stations, loads of them, with Netherbridge Halt buried somewhere in the middle. All at once Lottie stopped feeling miserable, and went back to being just plain angry. Netherbridge was a tiny little town in the depths of the country somewhere, and Mum was dumping her there. In fact, she wasn't even taking the time to dump Lottie in person, she was just putting her on the train, and leaving her uncle Jack to pick her up at the other end.

"I can't even remember what he looks like," Lottie muttered angrily to herself, blinking back tears. She had met him before, but it was ages ago, at a family party that her mum hadn't really wanted to go to. Lottie's mum didn't like being around Lottie's dad's family anymore. She said it made her feel too sad.

Uncle Jack was Lottie's dad's older brother, and he ran a pet shop in Netherbridge. Lottie had never been there, but she'd seen it in the photos Uncle Jack sent every year in his Christmas card. She had one, actually, in her bag. Mum had given it to her, so she would recognize Uncle Jack at the station. She rummaged through her bag, at last finding the photo wedged inside her book.

Uncle Jack looked very like the photos of Lottie's father. He had the same curly black hair that Lottie had inherited, and very dark eyes. Usually that would have fascinated her, but right now Lottie was less interested in her uncle than the shop behind him — where she was going to be living for the summer. Her mood lifted slightly. Lottie's mum had always been antipet, very much so. She said animals were messy and smelly, and wouldn't fit in an apartment. Even goldfish, which Lottie didn't think was very reasonable. It would be fun to be around some animals for once — it didn't look like Uncle Jack's was the boring sort of pet shop that only sold collars and cat toys. She peered carefully at the photo. It was hard to see much, but there seemed to be a parrot on a perch in the window, as well as bags of pet food. The sign above the shop said Grace's Pet Shop, and there was something else written underneath, but it was too small in the photo to see.

Grace's Pet Shop. It was quite nice to be going somewhere that had her own name written up above the door. Of course, it would have, Uncle Jack being her dad's brother. Lottie leaned back in her seat, staring dreamily out of the window and wondering what sort of animals the pet shop might have. Kittens, maybe? A small knot of excitement began to grow inside her — not that she was anywhere close to being happy about all this, of course not. She was furious. But there was no point in being so angry she didn't get to enjoy herself at all. It wasn't as if her mum would be around to see whether she was happy or not. Whenever she phoned, Lottie could quite easily be miserable.

Lottie was rather silent in the van on the way back to Uncle Jack's. She'd managed to forget on purpose that Uncle Jack's son, Danny, would be around, too — even after Mum kept going on about how nice it would be to get to know her cousin. Danny was only a year older than Lottie was, but he was a lot bigger than she, and extremely good-looking, and he seemed very sure of himself. Not that Lottie was shy, not normally, anyway, but it was hard to know what to say to him. Were they supposed to be friends just because they were related? Lottie supposed it was a bit weird for him, too, suddenly having a cousin he hardly knew dumped in his house. Danny wasn't unfriendly, but he just gazed out of the window and didn't talk, which made it even more noticeable that her uncle was trying very hard to keep the conversation going.

Uncle Jack's van smelled weird, Lottie thought, trying not to sniff too obviously. Maybe it was pet food? She jumped suddenly as something cold was pushed against her hand. Uncle Jack heard her gasp and turned around. The van swerved.

"Dad, watch it! You're driving!" Danny yelled.

"Sorry, sorry!" Uncle Jack murmured, waving apologetically at the driver of the car behind, who was looking a bit unnerved. "Don't worry, Lottie, it's just Sofie. She was asleep in there, I should have warned you."

Lottie looked down at the pile of blankets she was sitting next to. It was wriggling, and now a damp black nose emerged, followed by a pointed muzzle and a pair of liquid brown eyes. The little dog twitched her ginger eyebrows at Lottie, and lifted the side of her mouth in an unmistakable smile.

Danny looked over his seat, and let out a low whistle. "You're lucky, she likes you."

"How do you know?" Lottie asked, stroking Sofie's nose.

Danny turned back around, grinning. "She hasn't bitten your hand off."

Lottie gave the dog a doubtful look, and then frowned. It almost looked like Sofie had winked at her.

"Now, that's not fair," Uncle Jack disagreed. "All dachshunds are temperamental. Sofie's just choosy about the company she keeps."

"Yeah, tell that to the mailman. . . ." Danny said, smirking.

"He stepped on her!" Uncle Jack said indignantly.

Sofie swarmed her way out of the blankets and coiled herself into Lottie's lap, where she gazed up at her innocently. *Me . . . ?* she seemed to be saying. She was a beautiful dog, shiny black, with ginger paws and those amazing ginger eyebrows. She looked as though she'd been polished. She answered one question, anyway — it looked as though Lottie would get to spend the vacation with at least one animal.

They parked in a yard behind the pet shop, and went in the back way. Uncle Jack dropped Lottie's bags and went to turn over the Closed sign on the door, while Lottie looked around in amazement, still hugging Sofie tightly. She'd never imagined anything like this. The shop was in an odd, crooked little house on the main street — Lottie had had a brief glimpse of the front as they drove past. It was black and white, with a big, many-paned bay window that took up the whole of the narrow front. But it seemed somehow to be much larger on the inside, full of corners and alcoves and niches. Every inch was packed with cages and tanks, wedged together all the way up the walls. It was oddly silent, and Lottie had the disconcerting feeling that she was being watched — almost examined. Then she decided she must be imagining things as the shop was filled with the squeak and scuffle of hundreds of tiny creatures.

Uncle Jack turned back from the door, smiling. "Well, here you are, Lottie. Grace's Pet Shop. Otherwise known as the Mouse Emporium!"

Lottie sat on her new bed, looking around the bedroom. It was really sweet. It had obviously been a little girl's bedroom sometime before, because it had pink polka-dotted curtains and pale pink walls. The bedclothes had pink polka dots too. In fact, there was something very weird about those pink polka dots. Lottie was sure she'd seen them before somewhere. Maybe one of her friends had something similar. Although, to be honest, the whole room felt familiar. She leaned back against the wall, staring around thoughtfully. The room was right at the top of the house, so it had a sloping ceiling, and the window was oddly crooked. No one she knew had a bedroom like this. So why did it feel like she'd been here before?

"Lottie!" Her uncle was yelling up the stairs. "Come and have a snack!"

Lottie gave one last considering look around, shook her head, and went downstairs.

Uncle Jack and Danny were in the shop, sitting on stools by the counter with drinks and cookies.

"I still think we're never going to get away with it," Danny said, shrugging. "How can we?"

"We just need to be a bit careful, it might not be for long," Uncle Jack told him soothingly, but he looked worried.

"Well, how long is she staying? I don't get it, does her mum just not want her or something —" Then he saw Lottie coming and shut up, shoving a cookie into his mouth whole instead.

Uncle Jack looked very embarrassed. His ears turned red and he glared at Danny. "Lottie! Tea? Orange juice? Have a cookie!"

It was obvious they'd been talking about her. Lottie supposed it was only natural, but she couldn't help feeling hurt. Especially because Danny had summed up exactly what she felt. Lottie's mum's exciting career move to Paris was more important than her own daughter. Suddenly she was blinking back tears, and she stared very hard at one of the cages without really looking at what was in it.

"Do you like mice?" Uncle Jack asked hopefully, moving over to her.

"Yes," Lottie sniffed. It wasn't as if she'd ever really known any, but she was sure she did. Blinking again, she realized that the cage she was staring at so hard was full of beautiful little white mice, so tiny and delicate, with ruby red eyes. They were all looking at her interestedly. It was quite odd to be stared at by mice.

"A new face," Uncle Jack said rather hurriedly. "Very curious, mice. Always like to know what's going on. Don't you? Mmmm." He tapped the cage-front affectionately, and the mice skittered off.

Lottie looked around at some of the other cages. "You've got a lot of mice," she said in surprise. Several of the cages held mice, in all different colors. Lottie peered carefully at the cage on top. Were those mice *pink*?

"Oh, we specialize in mice." Uncle Jack quickly steered Lottie to a cageful of beautiful glossy black ones. "We *are* the Mouse Emporium. But we have almost everything else too. Kittens, rats, lizards, goldfinches. We had a scorpion until last week, he was *very* interesting." Uncle Jack looked thoughtful. "He was quite sneaky, though, kept getting out of his tank. Bit of a worry."

"Miracle we're still alive," Danny muttered.

Lottie squirmed, feeling suddenly itchy. She hoped none of the other pets were given to escaping. Especially not the small ones, with lots of legs . . .

"Your mum said you liked animals?" Uncle Jack suggested hopefully.

"Oh yes!" Lottie nodded. "Will I be allowed to help in the shop at all?" she asked shyly.

Uncle Jack looked like he wanted to hug her, and Danny gave a cough that sounded suspiciously like a snigger.

"Of *course* you can." Uncle Jack led her over to a large run, where four black kittens were playing on some tree branches that had been built into a sort of climbing frame. They had loads of toys too. In fact, all the animals in the shop seemed to have toys and lots of things to do. It was also the cleanest pet shop Lottie had ever seen. "Would you mind playing with these?" her uncle asked anxiously. "They need lots of handling, so as to get used to people, and it's one of those jobs that I just don't get time for."

Lottie grinned. She was getting the feeling she was going to enjoy this summer.

For someone who loved animals, Grace's Pet Shop was a great place to live. Uncle Jack's attitude toward keeping animals seemed to be that every creature in the place should be as happy as possible. Lottie had been to pet shops at home (Mum occasionally gave in, but she always made Lottie promise that she wouldn't even *ask* for anything, they were just visiting) and although she loved seeing the animals, and daydreaming about owning them, sometimes it was a bit depressing. The cages were so small, and the pets seemed so bored. But not here. Lottie came downstairs on her second day at Grace's to find Uncle Jack building a mouse maze on the breakfast table out of all the china in the cupboards.

But even though she was surrounded by animals, Lottie couldn't help feeling a bit lonely. Danny was only a year older than she, but it felt like a lot more. He was nice to her when he was there, but he was hanging out with his friends most of the time, and when he wasn't out he was texting them, or on the computer that lived in the tiny office next to the kitchen at the back of the shop.

With no chance of hanging out with Danny, Lottie really missed her friends. She could borrow the computer (when Danny wasn't glued to it) to chat to her friends Rachel and Hannah from school, but they were out together a lot of the time.

"Why don't you take Sofie for a walk?" Uncle Jack suggested the next morning, seeing Lottie wander sadly into the shop after Rachel had just said she had to go because she was going ice-skating.

"Can I?" Lottie sounded surprised. "On my own?" Mum would never let her do that.

"Why not? Go for a stroll. Don't let Sofie off the leash, though. She's got no common sense about roads at all." Uncle Jack glared at Sofie as he said this, and she gave a sharp yap, almost as though she'd understood him.

"I won't! Come on, Sofie." Lottie grabbed her stylish red leash, and Sofie marched to the door with her nose in the air, and stood waiting for Lottie to clip it on, looking like a little princess.

"Look after her, won't you!" Uncle Jack called.

Lottie turned around to promise that she would, and then stopped with her mouth half open. Uncle Jack hadn't been talking to her. He was looking anxiously at Sofie, almost as though he expected the little dog to answer. Then he caught Lottie staring at him, and laughed, a little embarrassed. "Well, Sofie knows all the walks around here. Don't let her get lost, Sofie!" This time he made it sound like a joke, but Lottie was sure he'd been perfectly serious before. She opened the shop door, looking down thoughtfully at Sofie. She did look like she knew exactly where she was going. After a couple of corners, Lottie was fairly sure that she was the one being taken for a walk here. Sofie walked perfectly to heel, but when Lottie tried to go the wrong way, she would stop dead and look at her accusingly. Lottie tried pulling her once, just a little, but it was amazing how a dog so small could apparently stick her paws to the ground and suddenly be made of solid lead. This was obviously a walk on Sofie's terms.

The little dachshund seemed to be giving Lottie a guided tour of the town. She had good taste too. She took Lottie through a really pretty park with a fountain and loads of grass for sunbathing on. There was a skateboarding area, too, but Sofie sniffed in disgust at that, and Lottie was inclined to agree. It was full of teenage boys messing around and doing stupid stunts.

Sofie walked her in a complete circle around the fountain, so that she could appreciate the cool spray blowing on her face, then led her back through some alleyways to the main street. She stopped meaningfully outside a sidewalk cafe, with a window full of gooey, chocolaty cakes, and eyed Lottie demandingly.

Lottie was a bit surprised to find herself apologizing to a dog. "I'm sorry, Sofie, I didn't bring my purse. Another day, though, I promise. It looks great." Then she noticed that a couple of girls her age sitting outside the cafe were giving her funny looks, so she glared back and whispered, "Come on, Sofie."

They were wandering up the main street, Lottie window-shopping and mentally spending the large allowance Mum had left her with (guilt money, Lottie called it), when she heard a clock chiming four. Surprised, she checked her watch. She and Sofie had been out for nearly two hours! The time had gone so quickly.

"We ought to go, Sofie. Thank you for a lovely walk, though." Lottie quickly checked that no one was near enough to hear her talking to a dog as though it could understand. "You really cheered me up." Lottie scooped up Sofie and gave one of her black satin ears a quick kiss. Then she put her down again and looked at her worriedly. Sofie was so proud, would she mind being kissed? She did look rather shocked, and Lottie hoped she hadn't insulted her. Then Sofie lifted one lip in an odd, slightly shy grin, one that lasted about two seconds before she shook her ears briskly and waltzed off, not waiting for Lottie to catch up.

Uncle Jack didn't seem bothered that they'd been out so long. In fact, Lottie wasn't actually convinced he'd noticed. He was sitting at the counter with Horace, the elderly African gray parrot whose perch was in the window. Horace liked to spend a certain amount of time sitting with his shoulders hunched up, watching the passersby. He seemed to really like it when they thought he wasn't real — then he had the satisfaction of shooting out his neck and hissing insults at them through the window, just when they'd decided he was stuffed. But in the afternoons he tended to wander around the shop, clinging on to the tops of the cages with his massive knobbly claws and suddenly swooping his head down to inspect the inhabitants. He particularly enjoyed giving the mice heart attacks by suddenly shouting rude words at them, peering around his cruelly hooked beak and hurr-hurring as they shot into their shelters.

Today he was sitting next to Uncle Jack, thoughtfully crunching a ballpoint pen. Uncle Jack had one too; he was tapping it against his teeth. "But if four down is Paracelsus, then that doesn't fit!" he was complaining as Lottie pushed open the door.

"Learn to spell," somebody said grumpily. "Sorcery, s-o-r-c-e-r-y, not s-a-u-c-e-r-y, idiot."

Lottie looked around for Danny, but he wasn't there. It was only Uncle Jack . . . and Horace the parrot, who was giving her a *look* that suggested he thought she was an idiot too.

"Uncle Jack . . ."

"Mmm?" Uncle Jack had now folded up the paper so the crossword didn't show, and was apparently deep in the business pages. Trying to look innocent, he blinked around the edge at Lottie.

"Was Horace . . . was Horace helping with the crossword?"

Her uncle's eyebrows shot up into his curly hair. He looked at Horace in amazement. "Horace? No! No-no-no-no-no." Uncle Jack smirked around the other side of the newspaper at the parrot, who had hopped back to his perch and was watching them grimly. "I would never ask Horace for help with the crossword," Uncle Jack said solemnly. Then he leaned forward conspiratorially. "Do you know why?" he whispered.

Lottie shook her head, feeling as though she might be about to be let into some deep dark secret.

"He's completely birdbrained!" Uncle Jack fell about laughing at his own joke, and Lottie sighed. She clearly wasn't going to get a straight answer.

"Oh, your mum called for you, Lottie," Uncle Jack suddenly remembered as she headed angrily for the stairs. "Said it was important and to call her back at the office."

Lottie stopped on the bottom step, looking back worriedly. She just had a feeling that this wasn't going to be good news.

Dialing through to Paris seemed to take a very long time, but eventually she got her mum on the other end. She sounded very cheerful, determinedly cheerful, as though nothing was going to get her down.

"Lottie! How's it going, sweetheart? Uncle Jack said you were out with Sofie? Is that a new friend? That's brilliant!"

Lottie sighed. She knew she'd told her mum that Sofie was a dog, but Mum was so busy with work that she really wasn't taking in a lot of what Lottie told her.

"Mmm." It was true anyway. She *did* feel like Sofie was a friend. Was it really sad to have a dog as your current best friend? Judging by those two girls at the cafe, there wasn't a lot of choice for Lottie around here anyway.

"I've got some great news, too, Lottie!" Mum was sounding really excited.

"Mmm?" Lottie's voice was guarded. Her ideal news would be that Mum was coming home, now. A tiny spark of hope started somewhere deep inside her, warming her. Lottie forgot about the fun she'd had with Sofie in a sudden rush of longing for home, the apartment, her school friends . . .

"They're really pleased with the work I've been doing over here, so pleased they want to extend the placement. Isn't that wonderful? It might mean that you have to change schools for the September term, but that would be all right, wouldn't it? You've already got one new friend. Does this Sofie go to the local school?"

"No," Lottie said dully, laying the phone — which was still squeaking with her mother's excitement — down on the bed. "No, she doesn't." And she got up and walked downstairs, trying not to skid on the slippery wooden treads, because she couldn't see through her tears.

"Are you sure you'll be all right?" Uncle Jack was looking at her anxiously. "I wouldn't leave you, but I need to pick up this delivery. It's quite important." He frowned. "I could ask Danny to stay with you!"

"No, you couldn't." Danny was sliding past the counter, smooth as a snake, making for the door. "Sorry, off to Ben's house. You said I could." And he was out, the shop bell jangling behind him.

"Danny!" Uncle Jack kept looking between where Danny had been standing and the door, as though he couldn't quite understand how Danny had managed it.

"It's fine," Lottie said tiredly. "You'll lock the shop

door, won't you? And you're only going to be half an hour. I'll probably go and watch some TV." More than anything, she just wanted to be left alone, but Uncle Jack had been fussing over her since she'd come back down.

"Well, I'll be as quick as I can," Uncle Jack agreed reluctantly.

Lottie leaned her elbows on the counter, gazing unseeingly at her book. Sofie was curled up under her stool, and Lottie could hear her sleepy breathing. It was a peaceful, comforting noise, murmuring under the squeaks and scuffles from the other animals. Lottie was worn out from crying, and it wasn't long before she fell asleep, too, resting her chin on her arms.

She woke up suddenly, and realized that the shop was getting dark. Surely Uncle Jack had been gone for more than half an hour? Moving cautiously in the half-light, Lottie went to peer out through the back door. No, the van was still gone. Sofie had trotted after her, and Lottie picked her up, feeling a little hurt. She'd said she didn't mind Uncle Jack going, but he'd promised to be back soon. Miserably, she felt her way along the wall to find the light switches.

Suddenly, she found herself with her nose pressed up against the white mice's cage. The mice hadn't noticed her and Sofie at all; they were far too busy. It was a little hard to see, but it looked as though they were gathered in a ring, like an audience. Two mice were in the middle, turning over and over, tangling their tails, clawing and spitting. It reminded Lottie of some boys she'd seen fighting in the playground at school, and she felt quite like their vice principal, Mrs. Dean, as she tapped on the glass. "Stop it! Hey!" The mice whirled around and stared at her in horror. "Don't be so mean!" Lottie added to the bigger of the two fighters, who was still standing on the little one's tail.

"Fighting never helped anyone, you know," she added, quoting Mrs. Dean as she went on feeling for the light switch.

"Huh! That's what you think!" said a small, squeaky sort of voice.

Lottie stopped dead. She felt Sofie grow very still in her arms, as though she'd stopped even breathing. She turned around slowly and stared back toward the mouse cage, but the ring of mice had disappeared. Now they were doing all the things mice should be doing. Three of them were desperately running nose-to-tail on their wheel, casting panicked looks over at Lottie. She could almost hear them muttering *"Yes! Can you see? We're just running on our wheel! Do it all the time! Nothing suspicious about us! Talk? Us? Never!"* The large mouse who had been fighting was being held down and sat on by three others, all frantically nibbling at sunflower seeds and trying to look natural.

Lottie shook her head. She'd just woken up. She was tired. It was nearly dark. There were hundreds of explanations for what had just happened.

Yes, she thought, but the most obvious one is that I just had a conversation with a mouse. . . .

Uncle Jack arrived back a couple of minutes later, very apologetic, to find Lottie still standing in the dark. Actually, he thought she'd gone to bed, and he jumped about a foot when he turned the lights on and saw her blinking at him.

"Lottie! Are you all right? What are you doing in the dark? Look, I'm really sorry I'm late. The delivery took ages. . . ." He trailed off, looking worriedly at her.

Lottie summoned up all her energy and smiled. "I'm fine." Then she frowned at him. "But you're all scratched! What happened?"

Her uncle rubbed a hand over his face, looking a bit shifty. "Oh. Yes, nothing to worry about. I . . . dropped something. . . ."

Lottie glared at him. Fine. Another secret. Everyone seemed to be keeping secrets from her these days. She stomped off upstairs, so angry that she almost forgot about the mice.

But not quite.

*   *   *

Lottie was just grateful that she had Sofie to talk to. They went on a lot of walks, and most afternoons they ended up at the sidewalk cafe and shared a cake. Lottie drank juice, but she always had to buy Sofie an espresso, thick syrupy black coffee. Sofie had sat with one perfectly polished black claw spearing the menu and glared at her until she asked for it. Lottie didn't even try to pretend it was for her anymore. Sofie had nearly disowned her the first time she tried putting the cup on the floor for the dachshund to drink. She sat on Lottie's lap and lapped delicately out of the cup, licking the tiny bubbles off her nose with a bright pink tongue. The waiter thought Sofie was great, and he always brought her an extra one of the little cookies that came with the coffee. Sofie graciously allowed him to stroke her in return.

Lottie really wasn't looking forward to going to school in Netherbridge. She'd seen a few girls her age around the town when she was out with Sofie, but none of them had looked very friendly, and certainly she hadn't met anyone who might replace Hannah and Rachel. Not that she wanted to replace them, of course. She *would* be going back home, and back to her old school. She might not even need to be at Netherbridge Hill school for a whole term. Hopefully.

It was a couple of weeks into Lottie's stay, and the hottest day so far. The pet shop's one downside as a place to live was that it didn't have a garden, just the little yard at the back. So the park was the only option for someone who wanted to spend the afternoon zoned out under a tree. She and Sofie loved to sunbathe there, and quite often spent an hour or so lying on a towel by the fountain. Lottie would lie on her tummy and read, or pretend to read while really she was snoozing, and Sofie would just snooze without trying to disguise it.

Lottie poked around the shop, gathering a book and a bottle of water and her sunglasses, and discovered that Sofie had put the red leather leash on her foot. Most dogs would have held it up in their mouths and looked pleading. Sofie managed to imply that Lottie should have put it on already, and could she get a move on, please.

Lottie grinned. "OK, then. Uncle Jack, can I take Sofie?"

Her uncle turned around from the large cage where he was cooing to the goldfinches. "Do you have a choice?" he asked, grinning.

Luckily the park was very quiet, and she and Sofie had their pick of the best spots. They chose a massive oak tree, which threw a lovely mottled shade on the soft grass. The heat and the gently waving leaves meant they were both dozing in less than ten minutes.

Lottie woke up to find Sofie's paws on her chest, and the dog's delicate but extremely cold nose in her ear. It was very effective.

"Ugh! Sofie, that's mean, I was asleep." Lottie sat up, shuddering.

Sofie just fluttered her eyelashes and rooted around in Lottie's straw bag, at last triumphantly pulling out her purse. Clearly, she wanted a cake. Or perhaps an ice cream.

"Actually, I could really go for an ice cream too," Lottie agreed, stretching sleepily. "All right. We'll wander back past the sweet shop, mmm?"

They were trailing slowly home, Lottie licking her ice cream and breaking off pieces of the cone to feed to Sofie, when they came around a corner and walked straight into a group of girls who looked about Lottie's age.

Lottie gulped. There were about six of them, and they didn't look friendly. "Hi," she murmured, quietly enough that if they just ignored her she could pretend she hadn't said anything in the first place.

None of them said anything. They just stared at her. Then one of them stepped forward slightly, a very pretty girl with long brown hair and a cool embroidered, sequinned skirt that made Lottie wish she wasn't wearing her old denim shorts. She looked Lottie up and down critically, and snorted. All the others giggled nastily.

"Your ice cream's dripping down your hand," the brown-haired girl said sweetly.

Lottie hadn't even noticed. Embarrassed, she tried to lick the dribbles off her fingers, and all the girls sniggered at her.

"You're that girl who's just moved here, aren't you? You're staying with Danny Grace and his dad?" one of the others said.

Lottie nodded. She wasn't sure how her voice would come out if she tried to talk. What was it about these girls that was so scary? Back home, she and Rachel and Hannah were some of the most popular girls in her class.

The one with the pretty skirt swung her hair back over her shoulders with a dismissive flick. "I heard you got dumped on Danny and his dad because your mum's run away, or something."

"She hasn't!" Lottie gasped angrily. "She's gone to France, for her job."

"And left you behind?"

"Yeah, why didn't she take you with her?"

"Zara's right, poor Danny, having you dumped on him!"

They were all chiming in now, ganging up on her, moving in closer.

Sofie growled, and Lottie wished she could too. She was furious with herself, but she could feel tears starting to burn the back of her eyes. Why did she do nothing but cry all the time right now? It was all Mum's fault. They were right, she *had* dumped her. Lottie sniffed desperately. She would not let them see her cry. She looked around for an escape route, a shop to dash into, or something, but there was nowhere to go. So she just whisked back around the corner, back the way they'd come, actually pulling Sofie with her for once. There were lots of ways from the park to the shop, they'd go back by one of those. And next time she saw those stupid girls, she'd have some really good answers ready for any mean stuff they said.

But she hadn't reckoned on them chasing her.

In fact, the girls probably wouldn't have done so, except that it was the summer vacation and they were already bored, and didn't have anything to do — and Lottie seemed like easy prey. *Obviously* she'd been about to cry. It would be fun to make her really lose it.

Lottie looked back in horror as she heard them giggling and calling as they raced after her, their feet thudding on the sidewalk. The whole group came piling around the corner after them, sniggering. Sofie took one look and set off at her surprisingly speedy bouncing run, dragging Lottie along behind her. She barked sharply at Lottie to get her to move, as she was still standing there looking like a frightened rabbit. The jerk of the leash brought her back to her senses, and she raced after Sofie, cursing herself for not having a smart answer, for running away like they'd wanted.

"Oh sorr-eee, did we make you cry?"

"Are you missing your mummy?"

"*Danny* says you're a real pain!"

Lottie and Sofie raced back the other way to the pet shop, the mean comments following them. Lottie didn't think those girls would dare chase them inside the shop, would they? She wasn't sure *what* they would do if they caught her, but she didn't want to find out. The group was only just behind them, and Lottie could feel that Sofie was slowing down. She was only tiny, and she couldn't keep up this speed for long. Lottie reached down and scooped her up, almost stumbling, but managing to keep going.

Suddenly Lottie realized they were coming to an intersection, and she wasn't sure if they had to go straight or turn to get back to the shop. Usually she just followed wherever Sofie was taking her. She cast an anxious glance back over her shoulder. The girls were so close behind, she didn't have time to be indecisive. Looking at the different roads, she vaguely thought she recognized the right-hand turn, an alleyway with high brick walls that looked like a shortcut that Sofie had taken her through before.

She started down the alley, but Sofie suddenly howled at her. "Nooo! Not zat way! Follow me, *imbécile!*" Then she jumped out of Lottie's arms and hurried back the other way, along the left-hand road.

The other girls shrieked with excitement as they saw their chance. They sped up again, one of them grabbing at Lottie and nearly pulling her bag off her shoulder. Lottie was still running as fast as she could, but her head was whirling, and it was hard to concentrate on their escape. She *really* hadn't imagined it this time. Sofie had told her which way to go — not just by meaningful looks or expressive barks. A dog had actually spoken to her. In a French accent.

Then the brown-haired girl, Zara, caught her wrist, and Lottie jerked to a stop, wrenching her hand away.

"Got you," Zara said triumphantly, as the rest of the girls caught up and stood in a bunch around them, trapping Lottie.

Lottie glared back at her, and Sofie shot back to let off a volley of high-pitched angry barks. Lottie stood there trying to look cool and not at all scared. It helped that some of her brain was still desperately trying to find an explanation for Sofie that didn't include a talking dog.

"Yeah. You did. So now what?" she asked snappily, hating the fact that her voice was trembly and hoping that it sounded like she was out of breath and not terrified.

Zara raised her perfect eyebrows. She'd been expecting Lottie to break down and howl, not answer back. This might be fun. "Don't you think it's a bit rude to run off in the middle of a conversation?" she purred.

Trying very hard to think of something to say, Lottie stared back at Zara, thankful that at least she had Sofie on her side. She might be tiny, but she was fierce. She was still barking those loud, sharp barks. Clearly she wasn't scared of the girls at all, and that made Lottie feel a lot braver.

"Hey!"

Lottie swung around, hearing feet hammering the sidewalk. Then she took a deep, shuddering breath of relief. Danny was racing up the street toward them, looking furious. Sofie stopped barking and sat down, her sides heaving with the effort she'd made, but her tail curled around her in a very smug sort of way. Had she been *calling* him?

"Zara Martin," said Danny disgustedly, as he shouldered his way past Zara's gang and planted himself firmly next to Lottie. "I might have known. Giving Lottie a friendly welcome, were you?"

Zara looked sulky. "We were just talking," she muttered.

Lottie looked around. It was an amazing transformation. All the girls were looking embarrassed, and seemed to be wishing themselves anywhere else but here. Then she suddenly got it. They were the same age as her, and Danny was the year above. They must all have been at Netherbridge Hill together until Danny graduated, and they had a crush on him. . . . She couldn't imagine liking Danny herself (urgh . . .), but he *was* good-looking. She tried not to smirk and didn't manage it.

"What are you grinning at?" Zara snapped, and Lottie stopped smiling. Even with Danny there, she was still scared of Zara — something about the way she spoke made Lottie feel small, and lonely.

"Leave her alone," Danny growled. "Get out of the way, you guys, we're going home." He put an arm around Lottie's shoulders and marched her off, leaving the girls muttering furiously. It sounded as though Zara was blaming everyone else for embarrassing her in front of Danny.

They walked in silence for a couple of minutes, and then Danny burst out huffily, "Well, you could say thank you, you know!"

Lottie stared at him. Now that she'd gotten away, she was remembering what had happened. "Sorry," she murmured. And then suddenly she sat down on the sidewalk, feeling dazed. It was all too weird. Talking dogs. Being chased by gangs of evil girls. She just wanted to go home.

"Hey, Lottie! Are you OK? Those little brats didn't hurt you, did they?" Danny was crouched down by her anxiously, and Sofie was clambering into her lap.

Lottie shook her head. She forgot that Danny was her cool older cousin, and that he was going to think she was lying, or crazy, or just plain stupid. She needed to tell someone. "Sofie talked," she told him in a flat voice. She was too worn out to explain properly.

"What?" he asked her sharply.

"She talked. She told me I was going the wrong way when they were chasing us. She said I was an imbecile. I think." Sadly, she looked up, expecting him to be laughing. She didn't care. It was true.

Danny wasn't laughing. He looked furious, and Lottie took a breath, scared, thinking he was going to have a go at her for lying to him, when he'd just saved her skin. But it wasn't her he was angry with.

"I knew it! Sofie, you stupid dog, can't you keep your mouth shut for five minutes? Don't you know how hard we've been trying to keep it a secret?" He sat down on the curb next to Lottie with a thump and sighed. "Not that it was *ever* going to work. Dad was just kidding himself."

Lottie gaped at him. "You mean, you *knew*?"

But Danny wasn't listening. Sofie had stood up on Lottie's lap and was shouting at him, her nose in his face. "And what was I supposed to do, huh? Let her run into a dead end and let those, those *vaches* catch us, yes?" Her voice was rich and husky, and extremely angry.

"No! But you could have told her without *telling* her! Oh, you know what I mean," he added irritably, when Sofie sniggered.

"You really do talk!" Lottie murmured wonder-ingly.

"Of course I do!" Sofie snapped, giving her an irritable look. "It is hardly difficult, *you* do it all the time."

31

She turned back to Danny. "It was never going to work. She is a nice girl, she has understanding. We tell your father, he will not mind."

"Huh! He'll be delighted." Danny grinned. "It's been killing him." He stood up, taking Sofie's leash. "Come on. Let's go home."

"Hey!" Lottie yelped, and they both turned back, looking surprised. She scrambled up. "You still haven't told me what's going on! *How* can Sofie talk? Is she — is she . . . ?" She didn't really want to say the word *magic*, it seemed too silly. But it also seemed to be the only word that fit.

Sofie looked up at her and smiled, showing all her teeth in a surprisingly wolfish grin from such a small dog. "*Magique*, Lottie? You can say it, it's allowed. No one will laugh."

Danny shrugged. "Yeah, she is. Look, Lottie, please can we just go back to the shop? Dad can explain it better than me."

Lottie shook her head in amazement. Danny just didn't seem to think it was anything that special. She trailed after him and Sofie as they headed back, still arguing with each other in whispers, Sofie doing a very good impression of a pretty but oh-so-normal dog when they passed anyone.

When they got back to the shop, Lottie had that feeling she'd had so many times before, that as the bell on the door jangled, every creature in the place held its breath for a second. Now she knew why. They were waiting — waiting to see if they needed to pretend. It was obvious now that she thought about it. All those little things that actually added up to one hugely enormous thing, if she'd ever sat down and properly thought it through. The mice in the top tank *were* pink, and that white mouse had spoken to her. Horace did tell Uncle Jack how to spell, and that day she couldn't find her new magazine anywhere, the black kittens in the big pen really had been reading it. Obviously they'd been doing the quiz on how to tell if you might be psychic. How could she ever have thought that this was just a normal pet shop? She glared at a white mouse who happened to be peeking out of the cage at her, and he jumped back, looking shocked. Lottie felt a teeny bit guilty, but then that mouse had been lying to her for days.

Uncle Jack was on the phone, enthusiastically ordering venomous lizards, and Danny was scribbling him a note, which he then waved in front of his dad's nose urgently. Uncle Jack squinted at it, and then gave Lottie a look of horror. She stared back angrily.

"Tomorrow? Yes, great," her uncle muttered, and he put the phone down rather nervously. "Hello, Lottie!" he tried cheerfully.

Lottie gave him the same glare she'd given the mouse, and Uncle Jack wilted slightly.

"I'm sorry, Lottie. What else could we do? When

your mother rang, I was so pleased. It was so long since we'd seen you — you were tiny last time — I thought it would be lovely to have you staying, and Danny could do with some company. And it wasn't until I'd said yes that I thought what I'd gotten myself into."

"You've all been lying to me," Lottie said, still trying to sound snappish. "I suppose Mum thinks it's really funny," she muttered, giving up and just letting herself sound miserable.

"Your mother?" Uncle Jack sounded surprised. "Oh, no, she doesn't know. Please don't tell her!" he added hurriedly.

"She is not *sympathique*," Sofie put in, shaking her head so her ears flapped. "She would not understand."

Lottie thought about her mum, so businesslike and sensible, and decided Sofie was right. She would laugh, and shake her head, and say that Lottie had always been so imaginative, in that way that made Lottie want to thump her. "You should have told me," she said sadly. "Didn't you think I would understand either?"

"How were we supposed to know?" Danny was sitting on the counter, staring down at her thoughtfully. "I couldn't remember what your name was, let alone if you were the sort of person it was safe to tell that we had a pet shop full of magic animals. Look, I can't even have people from school around in case some dumb dog blows our cover." He glared at Sofie, who made a dismissive hissing noise. "Then Dad goes and lets you come and live here!"

"We really were planning to tell you — eventually. . . ." Uncle Jack leaned over the counter toward Lottie. She couldn't help feeling like she was being interviewed, with him and Danny and Horace all looking at her like that. "We just had to see what sort of person you were. You were getting on so well with Sofie, that was a good sign."

"I kept telling zem you were a nice girl," Sofie said, putting her paws up on Lottie's legs. "Not everyone understands how I need coffee," she added resentfully, glaring at Danny, as Lottie picked her up.

"Oh, so you've been letting her have coffee?" Danny asked, rolling his eyes. "That explains why she's been so crazy recently. *And* why she can't keep her mouth shut."

"She buys me *espresso*," Sofie said smugly, licking Lottie's chin. "Like I say, she is a *very* nice girl."

"Soooo, we've just told Lottie the world's biggest secret because of a dog on a caffeine kick." Danny shook his head, mock-sad. "OK, we're dead." But he seemed to be seeing the funny side as well — he kept laughing to himself.

Uncle Jack sighed irritably. "Thank *you*, Daniel." He turned back to Lottie. "Lottie, I'm sorry we, well, that we lied to you, I suppose. But you have to understand. It's a big thing, a huge secret like this, it can — oh, weigh you down. Do you see what I mean? We really couldn't tell you straight away. Not until we knew you better." His apologetic smile widened to a big grin, reminding Lottie of her favorite picture of her father. "But I'm glad that you know now."

Lottie couldn't help smiling back. It was horrible, feeling like everyone had been lying to her, but she *could* see why they'd had to. And how could she be miserable now? She was surrounded by animals, like she'd always wanted — but she'd hardly dared to dream of anything as magical and wonderful as this.

When Lottie came downstairs the next morning, the shop felt completely different. All the animals were watching her again, but the wary, secretive atmosphere had gone. Now they were openly staring, and several of the mice were giggling. Lottie thought it was a bit like walking into a new school, and then she shuddered slightly.

"Hi, Lottie!" squeaked a particularly daring mouse, one of the pink ones in the very top cage. Then it collapsed in fits of giggles, and all the other pink mice chattered excitedly about how brave it was.

Lottie grinned. She fetched the stepladder they used to reach the high cages, and climbed up to see the pink mice better. Uncle Jack had always managed to shoo her out of the way whenever she'd been about to clean their cage out, so she'd never caught more than a glimpse of them — just enough to think that they really were a rather strange color.

"Oooh, she's coming up, she's coming. . . ." The pink mice rushed around their cage in a state of the jitters, practically bouncing off the walls.

Feeling suddenly shy, Lottie stopped with her nose just level with the cage. "Do you mind if I come up?" she asked nervously, peering up at the mice. Two of the bravest were standing on the large cardboard tube Uncle Jack had given them to play in, clinging to each other, with their tails twined around in a knot. They reminded Lottie of some of the ditzier girls at school, working themselves up over something really silly.

"Of course we don't mind," one of them chortled. "We've been dying to meet you."

"Oh yes, absolutely *dying* to . . ." said the other, her dark red eyes bulging with excitement.

By now the rest of the pink mice were creeping to the front of the cage, too, and all the other cages were rustling and squeaking as their owners woke up and popped out to see what was going on. Lottie giggled as she heard half a dozen squeaky comments on her hair, her choice of top (they didn't think green was her color, apparently), and the appalling state of her fingernails.

"Are you enjoying it here, Lottie?" a silvery little mouse asked, its head to one side, trying to look serious.

"Yes, we thought you looked quite sad sometimes," another agreed.

"Oh yes!"

"Yes!"

"You were putting us off our sunflower seeds, some days," the pink mouse who'd spoken to her first said.

"Sssshhh, don't say that, that's rude!"

"It isn't, it's true! I left a whole half sunflower seed that day she was crying! Hey! Don't tread on my tail like that!"

"Don't leave your tail lying around in other people's way, then. Honestly, I nearly broke my neck. . . ."

"You were the one who stepped on her! You did it on purpose!" a mouse from another cage squeaked. "I saw you!"

Lottie listened, fascinated, as they squabbled. They'd forgotten about her entirely.

"Ignore those silly little things," someone drawled, in a rather superior voice. "It's well known that pink mice don't have the sense they were born with. All looks and no brain." A large, glossy black rat was lounging languorously on top of his sleeping quarters. "Not that brown or white ones are really known for their IQ," he added.

"Oh, shut up, Septimus!" squeaked about half a dozen mice at once, breaking off their argument.

Septimus yawned, showing remarkably large and yellow teeth. He closed his eyes, then opened one again, and added to Lottie, "If you want any *useful*

information on rodent affairs, do drop in anytime. . . ."
Then he appeared to go back to sleep, leaving Lottie
feeling as though she'd been dismissed.

"Just humor him," one of the pink mice hissed. "He
thinks he's in charge. See you later, Lottie!" Then they
all fell about laughing again.

Lottie climbed down the ladder and wandered into
the kitchen, trying to work out how the mice had managed to keep themselves relatively quiet for over a
week. She was seriously wondering if Uncle Jack had
put a spell on them, she couldn't see anything else
working.

Breakfast was wonderful. Lottie didn't have to sit
staring silently at her cereal and trying to think of
things to say to Danny. Instead she listened to the low
hum of chatter from the shop, trying to pick out the
different voices. She'd only managed to meet a few of
the animals the day before, and now she couldn't wait
to talk to them all.

Sofie sat beside her on a pile of purple cushions, her
front paws on the table. Uncle Jack had made coffee
and poured her a beautiful pink china bowl of it. She
was sipping blissfully, her tongue just a slightly darker
shade of pink than the bowl.

Danny lounged in his seat and glared at Sofie, her
muzzle wreathed in coffee steam. "I thought we weren't
giving her coffee?" he complained. "I don't want her
bouncing off the walls all day."

Sofie wrinkled her nose scornfully. "As if you would be here, anyway, *mon petit chou*. Off with your little friends straight after breakfast, hmmm?"

Danny shrugged, grinning, and Uncle Jack shook his head. "Again? Aren't you going to spend any of the vacation here?" He was smiling, but Lottie thought he looked sad. She looked sideways at Danny, who was playing with his cell phone. She had a feeling he'd only taken it out as a distraction.

It was pretty clear that Uncle Jack and Danny had some kind of thing going on — that her uncle wanted Danny to be more involved in the shop, but Danny wasn't having it. Weird. How could anyone not want to be here *all the time*?

Resolving to ask Sofie about it — along with about a million other things, Lottie crunched happily into her toast.

Lottie sat behind the counter and waited hopefully for some customers. Surely a magic pet shop ought to be full of the most interesting people?

"Ow!" Uncle Jack trapped his fingers again. The cash register seemed to have a mind of its own, and slammed shut whenever he tried to take any money *out*. He was trying to show Lottie how it worked, but Lottie wasn't sure she wanted to risk it.

"I don't believe it, I'm actually bleeding!" Uncle Jack glared at the cash register. "I'll send you back, you know. Lottie, I'm just running upstairs to get a Band-Aid, all right?" He strode off, muttering.

Lottie tried hard to look sympathetic and not giggle, and then looked up eagerly as the shop door swung open. So far, the customers had just been people who wanted some dog biscuits, or flea powder (interestingly, Lottie discovered, they almost always bought the expensive kind that didn't work, instead of Uncle Jack's homemade version in the blue jars, which guaranteed every flea in a two-mile radius would be on its back within half an hour. Lottie reckoned he needed snazzier labels).

A smartly dressed woman walked in with her little girl, wrinkling her nose as though the shop smelled. She looked Lottie up and down rudely, and snapped, "Are you in charge?"

In spite of the woman's horrible voice, a little glow of pleasure filled Lottie. She came out from behind the counter, smiled politely, and said, "Yes, for the moment. Are you looking for anything in particular —"

The little girl, who looked about four, hit Lottie in the stomach with her very expensive-looking miniature handbag. "I want a mouse. Mummy says I can. I want one now!"

Anxious squeaks came from the cage by Lottie's head.

"Not me!"

"I'd rather you fed me to the kittens!"

42

"Ssshhh!" Lottie hissed out of the corner of her mouth. She smiled at the mother. "Um, are you sure? She's a bit young. . . ."

The woman glared back at her. "Is this a shop or not? I want to buy a mouse. And a cage. Whatever else we need. Just put it all in a bag."

There was a sudden outraged squawking and Lottie looked around to see that the little girl was trying to pull the feathers out of Horace's tail. Sofie was already making a quick getaway up the stairs.

"OK!" Anything to get rid of them, Lottie thought. She would find them a nice quiet mouse. She would sell them a very big, very expensive cage, and the mouse could hide in it. She took the little girl's hand. "Let's choose a mouse, shall we?"

"I want that one!" the little girl squealed, pointing into a cage Lottie had been sure was empty. She peered in, and saw a very sweet mouse the color of dark chocolate gazing back at her, its long whiskers wobbling.

"Um, not that one . . ." Lottie murmured, suddenly feeling too guilty. She couldn't do it to the poor little thing. She looked around desperately to see if Uncle Jack was coming.

"I *want* that one!" shrieked the little girl, hitting Lottie with her bag again.

Lottie was staring anxiously at the mouse, wondering if she should just go and *fetch* Uncle Jack, however silly she'd feel, when it winked at her. Most definitely.

"Mummy, she won't let me have my mouse!" the little girl was yelling now, and while she wasn't looking, the mouse crept closer to the bars and whispered, "Don't worry. You sell me to them. It'll be fun!"

Lottie gaped at the mouse, and shrugged. The mouse knew an awful lot more about how the shop worked than she did, she decided.

"Oh, *this* mouse! This one here? Of course you can have this mouse!" she said, hoping she was doing the right thing. "Now, you'll need a cage, and food bowls, a sleeping shelter . . ." She led them around the shop, piling up as much stuff as she could, and every so often casting a worried glance back at the chocolaty mouse, who nodded encouragingly. Lottie couldn't help thinking that she seemed a lot brighter than most of the others.

Lottie was just closing the door behind them (luckily the woman had given her the right money and she hadn't had to brave the cash register) when Uncle Jack appeared, looking as though he was trying not to laugh.

"Where have you been?" Lottie squawked. "I've just sold them a mouse, a really sweet one, she was in this cage here, but the little girl said she was going to dress her up and put her in the doll's house. I think we should go and get her back!"

"Lottie, Lottie, calm down," Uncle Jack said soothingly.

"She'll torture it!" Lottie wailed.

Uncle Jack patted her shoulder. "Don't panic. In this cage, yes? What color did you say she was?"

"Chocolate. With long whiskers." Lottie stared at the cage, looking puzzled. "The funny thing is, I could have sworn that cage was empty when I went around doing the water bottles earlier."

"Yes, well, Henrietta likes her personal space," Uncle Jack replied absently. "She probably didn't want you to see her. I've never seen her be chocolate colored before, she's usually white. Probably the child was chocolate-obsessed. That was very clever of Henrietta."

Lottie narrowed her eyes and glared at him.

"That was Henrietta the homing mouse, Lottie. I only sell her occasionally, to customers I really don't like, but obviously she recognized someone who needed her. She'll tell us about it when she gets back. Tomorrow, or early next week, maybe. It depends how long it takes her to chew through all the electric wires in the house."

"You mean, you sell her to people, and then she comes back?" Lottie asked, feeling confused.

"Well, yes, Lottie." Uncle Jack sounded as though he thought it ought to be obvious. "From what I heard when I was lurking on the stairs" — here he beamed at Lottie — "that little fiend shouldn't be within six feet of another living creature. And once Henrietta's finished, her parents will never even consider buying her another pet. Ever."

"What will she do?" Lottie asked slowly.

"Oh, well, she always likes to gnaw a couple of cables, she says that gives excellent results for very little effort, but she's a real professional. She likes to provide a tailor-made service, whatever will be most upsetting. You know, holes in the new sofa. Artistic arrangements of mouse poo in the cookie jar — especially if it's chocolate chip cookies. We'll have to wait and see."

The shop doorbell clanged, and Uncle Jack turned to welcome the new customer, leaving Lottie wondering if she was ever going to get used to this. She sighed, and stared hopefully at the very normal-looking old lady, who had tottered in to buy treats for her fat little dog and stopped to gossip with Uncle Jack. Lottie waited for details of spells, or owls, or *something* interesting, but all she wanted to talk about were her terrible problems with her feet.

Now that she knew what was really going on, Lottie wondered how people managed to come in for a bag of cat food and not realize what was going on at Grace's. "How could she not notice?" Lottie demanded ten minutes later, perching herself on the counter next to Uncle Jack. "Horace was making rude comments about her purple hair dye the whole time she was paying!"

Horace sniggered, and spat a sunflower seed at Lottie.

Uncle Jack shrugged. "She's been coming here for years, Lottie." He waved a hand vaguely around the shop. "It's a pet shop — it looks like a pet shop, smells like a pet shop. Why would anyone suspect anything else?" He glared at Horace. "Even when the mouthy bird can't keep his beak shut!" Then he gave Lottie a thoughtful look. "You'd be amazed, Lottie, what people can ignore if they want to. Most of the world is so desperate to be *normal*, and not to get involved in anything weird. The mice would have to be dancing the conga across the counter before anyone commented." His eyes sharpened up, fixing on hers. "You were noticing things, of course. You saw the scratches I got from those new invisible parakeets I went to see, for a start. Danny and I, we knew we weren't going to be able to keep it a secret for much longer. But then, it's in your blood. After all, your dad —"

Another customer came in then, interrupting them, and somehow, Lottie couldn't seem to get Uncle Jack back on the subject afterward, however hard she tried. He just kept distracting her. It made her wonder what else he could do too.

By the afternoon, Lottie was bursting with questions about the shop. It hadn't taken her long to realize that magical animals could have their downsides.

It was quite clear that Sofie's bossiness was something that most magical creatures shared, *especially* the cats. The four black kittens that Uncle Jack had asked her to play with on her first morning at the shop were awful. They had been bad enough when they could only meow, but now that they could actually talk to Lottie, they'd spent the whole morning ordering her about. They seemed to regard her as their personal slave, and they complained shrilly if she so much as looked at Sofie, who they hated.

"Lott-eeeee!" It was Selina's shrill meow *again*. Lottie wasn't sure if she was the worst, or whether Midnight, the biggest of them, won just by sheer rudeness. They all seemed to regard humans as an inferior species, designed only to open cans. "Lottie, I want a cat treat."

"You'll get fat. Oh, OK, just one."

"Me too! Me! Me!" The other kittens swarmed to the front of the pen, doing their best starving-to-death expressions.

"What's the magic word?" Lottie asked, without really thinking. It was like talking to a bunch of three-year-olds.

Selina wrinkled her delicate little muzzle in a smirk, looking sideways at her brothers. "Now!" they chorused in a yowl.

Lottie was really hoping that someone would buy them soon. She stuffed a handful of cat treats into the kittens' pen, and made a quick getaway. They were too busy fighting over them to notice. She slipped back into the kitchen to find Sofie, feeling as though she simply had to get a few more answers.

Sofie was curled on her cushion, pretending to be asleep. When she saw Lottie she opened one eye to see if she had food, then hurriedly shut it again.

"Wake up," Lottie said firmly. "I need to talk to someone, Sofie, please!" Then she resorted to bribery. "Look, Sofie, Mum sent me some French chocolates. . . ."

Sofie's sinuous curls unwound so fast she almost slipped off the chair, and she'd gulped the chocolate almost before Lottie got her fingers out of the way.

Lottie smiled to herself. She had a feeling that now she'd paid for some information. She tempted Sofie up to her room with the promise of more chocolates, and they settled on her bed.

"What do you want to know?" Sofie asked in a long-suffering voice.

Lottie gave her a surprised look.

"Lottie, I am not stupid, and you are bribing me with chocolate." Sofie fluttered her eyelashes. "It is very good chocolate, and bribery works on me very well," she added hopefully.

Lottie gave her another truffle. "Sofie, I need someone to explain everything!" she begged. "All Uncle Jack really told me yesterday was that the animals in the shop could talk, and I was so surprised, I didn't ask any questions. . . ." Lottie trailed off, not knowing how to begin. "I don't know *anything*," she said eventually. "Is there magic all over the place?"

Sofie looked thoughtful. "I suppose," she agreed. "It is not obvious, sometimes . . ."

Lottie looked at her. "Do you need more chocolate? Are you being mysterious on purpose?"

Sofie shrugged, very impressively for someone with such small shoulders. "Lottie," she whispered earnestly. "It is just a mysterious thing. Can I have another chocolate?"

Lottie sighed. She put the box down in front of Sofie, who settled down to read the flowery French descriptions of the centers with great seriousness. She was dithering between a champagne truffle and a lemon mousse when Uncle Jack called up the stairs. "Lottie! Henrietta's back! Do you want to hear what happened?"

Sofie gave the chocolates a panicked look, and Lottie grabbed them. "You can have them both, come on!"

They raced down the stairs, and Lottie noticed again that Sofie galloped down the steep treads far faster than she ought to be able to. Were her paws even touching the boards?

They skidded into the main room of the shop, and found Henrietta sitting on the counter, looking very pleased with herself. She was still a beautiful chocolaty brown, like cocoa powder.

"Hello, Lottie!" she said sweetly. "It is nice, isn't it, this color? I might stay like this for a while. Don't you think it sets off my whiskers?" She wrinkled her nose so that her amazingly long whiskers fluttered charmingly.

Uncle Jack came in from the kitchen with mugs of tea, including a thimbleful for Henrietta, and sat down behind the counter. "Come on, then!" he said eagerly. "What did you do? It must have been pretty spectacular, we weren't expecting you back for at least a couple of days."

Henrietta daintily sipped from the thimble, carefully holding her whiskers out of the way. "Ah, well, you see, it was rather a special occasion. Mrs. Delamere — that was the lady you met, Lottie — had taken little Louisa out shopping to get her out of the way. They live in that big house down by the river, you know, the one with the curtains that look like pink frilly underwear. More money than sense. Anyway, they were having a lunch party, very nice, caterers, flowers, the lot." Henrietta drank some more tea, savoring the memory. "Louisa *somehow* forgot to shut the door of my cage, so I went to investigate the dining room. For some reason it rather put all those ladies off their food when I popped out of the flower arrangement in the middle of the dessert course. Poor Mrs. Delamere managed to get herself covered in cream. She was quite upset."

Uncle Jack chuckled to himself.

"You know," Henrietta added thoughtfully, "they still think I'm in the house somewhere. This could be an ideal opportunity to get rid of one of those awful black kittens. . . ."

5

A few days later, a young woman walked into the shop while Lottie was minding the counter. Lottie blinked at her, confused. Had the bell on the shop door rung? All at once, Lottie could hear the echo of it in her mind, but it wasn't quite right, somehow . . . it was as though the woman had just *appeared* by the counter, but that wasn't possible. Lottie shook her head, feeling a little dazed.

She tried to work out if the woman knew what sort of shop she was in. She *looked* a little strange. Despite the heat, she was wearing a long black dress, the sleeves falling halfway down her hands, but she didn't look hot at all. She had pale, transparent-looking skin, and her hair was red, and long, and very straight. Lottie had tried her friend Rachel's flat iron a few times, and this was what she had been aiming for. It never worked.

The red-haired lady looked around, chirping pleasantly to some of the mice, and casting admiring glances at Uncle Jack's new venomous lizards, who were sunbathing under the very expensive lamp he'd bought them. It seemed to turn them an even viler shade of green. Then she turned to Lottie, looking her up and down too. Lottie felt as though someone had just turned her inside out — she began to suspect that this customer definitely wasn't just after a dog collar.

"I'm looking for a kitten," the lady said in a low, sweet voice. "Do you have any at the moment?"

"Ariadne! Hey, you're back! Dad will be over the moon." Danny shut the shop door with a bang, and hurried over to give the new customer a hug. Lottie looked at him in amazement. She'd never seen him hug *anyone*.

"Did you say you were looking for a kitten?" he asked, sounding interested. "What's happened? Is Shadow OK?"

Danny's friend smiled, a little sadly. "Oh, Danny, he's an old cat. He's retiring. I need to start training his replacement."

Lottie was listening hungrily. A cat, retiring? For a moment, all she could think of were guide dogs, and somehow she couldn't see a guide cat working very well. Then the explanation hit her, and she felt stupid, and a little scared.

This was a witch.

Lottie gasped. She couldn't help it. She had somehow thought that the magical customers would all be like Uncle Jack and Danny, normal-ish people. She'd met a few now, and they'd been very nice — almost disappointingly nice. She'd imagined them having boring sorts of jobs, in offices, and being glad to get home and have a chat with their pet rabbits. She hadn't gotten her head around *witches*, not at all.

The witch turned and looked at her, a little surprised, and Lottie flushed scarlet, which just made her feel more embarrassed than ever.

Danny was grinning. "Sorry. This is my cousin. She's new, only been here a couple of weeks. She's still getting used to us, aren't you, Lottie?" He smirked at her, and Lottie felt like hitting him.

"I'm sorry," she murmured, not looking at the witch. And then she added, "The kittens are in the next room!" hoping that everyone would just go away and leave her to look like an idiot in private.

"Could you show me?" the witch asked, her voice sweeter than ever.

Lottie could hear the enchantments working in the voice, telling her it was all right, not to be scared, there was no harm . . . it wove itself around her mind and made her feel dazed, and happy. Lottie shook her head slightly, and stared accusingly back, looking into the witch's eyes for the first time. They were green.

"Clever girl. You noticed that I didn't come in the front door, as well, didn't you?" The witch smiled at her again, and this time her voice sounded real, and amused. "But really, I only wanted you not to be scared."

"I'm not," Lottie said firmly. "Thank you." She got up and marched into the other room, hoping not to be turned into something horrible. The witch just followed her, and exclaimed delightedly when she saw the kittens.

"What perfect black coats!"

It took the kittens about three seconds to work out that this was a possible new owner that they actually wanted. Several old ladies had cooed over them admiringly, but they were very good at putting people off. They could lick their rear ends more thoroughly than any cat Lottie had ever seen.

Today they were in top form, whiskers sparkling with excitement. They settled themselves in a neat row in the middle of the pen, and curled their tails around their legs. Lottie grinned. Of course, they would never do anything as undignified as beg for attention, but she could see they were all dying to scream, "Me! Pick me! Me!"

Midnight glared at Lottie. "Our pen is dirty!" he hissed out of the corner of his mouth.

It wasn't, but Lottie whispered, "Sorry!" anyway. It was no use arguing with him.

"May I pick them up?" the witch asked Lottie politely.

"Oh! Yes, I'm sure that's all right. If they don't mind, I mean," Lottie stammered.

Selina, one of the girl kittens, gave her a pitying look. "I would love to be picked up. . . ." she purred, strolling to the front of the pen and flitting her whiskers. The others stared hatefully at her.

Lottie opened the pen door, and Selina oozed out. When the witch picked her up, she curled her tail around the black sleeve of her dress like a monkey, and rubbed her head adoringly along the witch's chin.

"Very charming . . ." the witch said thoughtfully. "Could be useful."

A flare of triumph shone in Selina's huge green eyes, but she closed them hurriedly when she saw Lottie watching her. She purred her remarkably charming purr.

The witch examined all the kittens, and seemed impressed. "Have they had any training yet?" she asked Lottie, who wasn't quite sure what she meant.

"No," growled Midnight. It was obviously a sore point.

"You're too young, Midnight." Uncle Jack had surfaced from the storeroom, and was standing behind them. "You know that perfectly well. And you needn't give me that look, I'm not changing my mind." He kissed the witch's cheek, and Lottie watched, wheels whirring in her mind as she struggled to keep up. This was a witch, and it looked very like she was also Uncle Jack's girlfriend.

"You're back sooner than you thought, love. You didn't bring Shadow?"

The witch kissed him back, and gave a little shrug. "Shadow knows I've come to look at kittens, and he doesn't want to retire. He's back at home, sulking. I do hope he snaps out of it soon, it's so much harder to train a new cat when the old one won't help."

All the kittens gave her their best "helpful and obedient" looks, and Lottie snorted with a laugh she couldn't hold back.

Ariadne chuckled too. "I think you're right. They're certainly very good at putting on a show. It *is* a pity Shadow wouldn't come, I'd have liked his opinion. Hmmm." She gazed thoughtfully at the kittens, who stared soulfully back. Then she sighed and turned to Uncle Jack. "I just don't know, Jack. I need to persuade Shadow to have a look at them too."

Uncle Jack nodded. "Don't worry. That lot aren't going anywhere. Come and have a cup of tea, tell me about your trip. You'll mind the shop, won't you, Lottie? We'll just be in the kitchen. Oh, hang on. Here." He handed Ariadne a pink sugar mouse from a drawer in the counter. "Shadow's favorite."

"Good idea, it might cheer him up." She peered back into the other room and cast one last considering look over the kittens, who thought she'd gone and had started to hiss boasts about who had impressed the witch the most.

Ariadne sighed. "Mmmm. Oh well. We'll see. Nice to meet you, Lottie." She smiled, and Lottie gazed after her. Ariadne's smile seemed to stay in the room, floating in the air, making Lottie feel impossibly happy.

How does she do that? Lottie wondered. And could anyone show me the secret?

6

"She says she bought it in Galeries Lafayette. Am I saying that right?"

"No. But do not worry about it. You are saying it as well as an English person can."

Lottie grinned down at Sofie, who was sniffing the parcel wistfully, and went back to the card of the Eiffel Tower that her mum had put in. "It's near where she works, apparently."

"Ah, L'Opera. Your mother's office is around there, yes? Good for shopping."

"What's it like, Paris?" Lottie asked, unfolding the T-shirt that her mum had sent her and laying it on her bed. It was gorgeous, pink with beaded butterflies scattered over it. Two of the pink mice, who'd coaxed Lottie into letting them come upstairs for a while, stopped chasing each other around the bed and stopped to admire it.

Sofie didn't answer for a moment. "Zat is a silly question," she said finally. She seemed to be sounding extra French since the parcel had come. "You might as well say, what is music like? It is all different."

"I suppose so," Lottie said apologetically. She wasn't sure if Sofie wanted to talk about Paris or if it made her homesick.

"She went up the Tour Eiffel?" Sofie asked, looking at the card.

"Yes." Lottie nodded, still reading. "She says it made her feel sick."

"Me, I agree. Ugly great thing. There is a story about a writer, zat he used to eat his lunch at the restaurant inside the Tower every day, because it was the only place in Paris he did not have to look at the Tower. She should go to the Sacre Coeur, now zat is beautiful." Sofie sighed, and laid her head mournfully on Lottie's knee. Its warm weight was very comforting.

"I'll tell her. I'll have to say that Uncle Jack's been there, or something. Or I guess I could say my friend Sofie, she's already forgotten you're a dog anyway." Lottie shrugged, trying not to sound hurt. She felt as well as saw Sofie's ears prick up, and a knot suddenly appeared in her chest. "We are friends, aren't we?" she asked in a small voice.

Sofie rolled over, showing her pinkish tummy. "Lottie, you are not a dog, so you do not know, but this is a thing to do that says you trust someone. I do not do it very often, because it looks silly. You may stroke me."

Lottie gently rubbed her tummy, and Sofie closed her eyes blissfully, her ears flopping back. After a moment, Lottie asked, "Sofie, how come you live here now, when you were born in France?"

"The French threw her out!" one of the mice chirped, rolling onto her back and giggling hysterically at her own joke.

Sofie made a snapping noise with her teeth, nowhere near the mice, but just close enough to make it clear that she could swallow them in one mouthful if she happened to feel like it. They disappeared under the bed, squeaking.

"I lived in Paris, at a shop like this one, for a while. Then your uncle brought me over here. I like it, it is a good place to live. Obviously, not as good as Paris," she added, in case Lottie was in any doubt.

"But how did Uncle Jack know about you? I mean, if you lived in France?"

"Lottie, think!" Sofie opened one eye to glare at her. "How many shops like this do you think zere are? There is only one magic pet shop in Paris, the one where I was born. Your uncle, he knows the owner very well. When he heard they had a dachshund, he bought me, as a present for his wife."

"His wife!" Lottie stared at her. "You mean, Danny's *mother*?"

"Of course." Sofie nodded. "She had very good taste."

From under the bed came the sound of shrill, mocking laughter.

Lottie felt stupid. For some reason, she'd never even thought about Danny's mum. Maybe because *she* only had one parent, it had just seemed normal. "Is she, um . . ."

"She died," Sofie said matter-of-factly. "Three years ago. Danny will not talk about her. He is still very angry that your uncle could not make her well, and that is why he does not want to do anything with magic."

"Oh." It wasn't a very good answer, but Lottie could think of nothing else to say. She started to change into the butterfly T-shirt, to give herself something to do.

Sofie nodded approvingly. "Nice. Very French. Very *chic*."

"Pink!" The mice peeped out from under the bed and nodded approvingly.

Lottie twisted in front of the mirror, feeling pleased. Then she sighed. Mum's card hadn't mentioned whether she'd be able to come and visit anytime soon, and she was really missing her.

"Lottie!" A soft voice called her, and Lottie jumped. Ariadne peered around the bedroom door. "Sorry, Lottie. I was calling, but you didn't hear. Jack's making tea, do you want some?"

"Oh! Yes, thanks!" Lottie gripped the hem of her new T-shirt nervously. She still found Ariadne worrying to be around, even though she was at the shop most days. It wasn't that Lottie was scared of her; Ariadne was fascinating. But Lottie could never think of anything to say when Ariadne spoke to her, and she had a horrible feeling Ariadne thought she was stupid, or boring anyway. Which was awful, because Lottie had never wanted to impress anyone so much in her life.

"That's a lovely top," Ariadne said, smiling. "Is it new? I haven't seen anything like it around here."

"My mum sent it. From Paris," Lottie whispered.

"That's in France!" one of the mice chirped obligingly.

"You look beautiful." There were no sweet enchantments in Ariadne's voice this time, she just sounded truthful. And nice.

Lottie's eyes filled with tears. It wasn't fair. She wished her mum could see her and tell her things like that.

"Hey, Lottie, that wasn't meant to make you cry!" Ariadne put an arm around her, and Lottie jumped. "It's OK, I won't put a spell on you, or anything like that. I want to help. What's wrong?"

Lottie sniffed and gulped and couldn't get any words out.

"Her mother sent her the top," Sofie explained. "Lottie misses her."

Ariadne sat down with them both on Lottie's bed. "I should think she misses you too," she suggested gently. "But she has to be away for work, doesn't she?"

Lottie shook her head. "I bet she could come home if

she wanted to," she muttered. "Sofie just told me about Danny's mum — and it's stupid, but I feel jealous of him," she gasped out, hating herself as she said it. "Danny still has his dad, and I know he lost his mum, but at least he knows she didn't leave him behind on purpose!" She glared at Sofie and Ariadne, expecting them to hate her, too, but Ariadne gave her a hug, and Sofie licked her face lovingly. The two pink mice hugged each other and said, "Aaahhhh . . ."

Ariadne sighed. "Your mum must have her reasons, Lottie. I wish I could make it all better for you, but not even magic can do that."

7

The black kittens had decided to blame Lottie for Ariadne not taking one of them home. The fact that it had been nothing to do with her didn't discourage them at all. They were prickly, and furious. The only time they behaved nicely was when Ariadne dropped in to see Uncle Jack, then they suddenly turned perfect. Lottie just wished she would stay longer. Whenever customers came into the shop, the kittens simply stared at them, until they suddenly remembered something else they were supposed to be doing and left in a hurry. Then the kittens would exchange a satisfied look before they went back to their grumpy bickering. Lottie wondered if they had magical abilities already, even though they hadn't been trained, but Uncle Jack said that staring people down was just a natural cat thing.

Sofie couldn't resist teasing them. She sat by their pen and told them long stories about famous witches' cats, occasionally looking at the kittens and sighing sadly. They grew edgier and edgier, until at last Selina took her revenge.

"Sofie, look, I have a new trick," she purred.

Sofie looked up at her sharply. "A trick? You are not supposed to do tricks. You are only kittens," she said disapprovingly.

"But it's such a good trick, come and see," Selina begged silkily.

Sofie foolishly stuck her narrow muzzle into the pen. Then she jumped back whining as Selina raked her claws down her velvety nose.

"There! That's my trick, now leave us alone!" Selina spat. "We are more magical than you will ever be, you stupid . . . dog!" Obviously, it was the worst insult she could think of.

The kittens jeered and chuckled, united for once, and Sofie scuttled out, a pattern of pink lines oozing across her nose.

"Those . . . evil ones! Criminals! Mouse-eaters! They should be drowned!" she snarled to Lottie, so angry she was actually spitting, something she was usually far too ladylike to do.

"You *were* teasing them," Lottie pointed out, reasonably enough.

"Ha! So you think it is fine for them to assault me, yes?" Sofie growled, showing her teeth. Lottie had a feeling that Sofie was taking her fury with the cats out on her.

"No, of course not!" she sighed. "Look, do you want some coffee? It might make you feel better." She started to head for the kitchen to put the coffeepot on.

Sofie put her head to one side, eyeing Lottie in a thoughtful way. *"Espresso?"* she asked slyly. "And a *cake*, Lottie?"

"Oh, all right. Let's go to Valentin's, then. I could do with getting away from the brat cats too." Lottie grabbed her purse.

"You will have to carry me," Sofie said in a weak voice. "I am injured." She held up one paw in a feeble way.

Lottie grinned. Sofie was such an actress. She would do anything for cake.

Two espressos had a remarkable effect on Sofie's mood, and on her scratches.

"They've gone!" Lottie said, almost accusingly, staring at Sofie's nose, which was nearly back to its usual smooth velvetiness.

Sofie nodded. "I know, I am surprised. I would not put it past that little *monstre* to have poison-claws, but it seems not."

Lottie stared at her. She supposed it wasn't that surprising — if Sofie could talk, why shouldn't she have other magical powers? Sometimes she wondered if there was more to the shop than Uncle Jack let her see. It all seemed so sweet and gentle — Uncle Jack liked to give the impression that the flea powders and dog tonics were just herbs, made from old recipes — but actually, Lottie was sure there was more to it than that.

Especially since she'd met Ariadne, who was so obviously a powerful witch. Was Uncle Jack actually a — well, a sorcerer, a wizard, a *what*? And how many others like him were there around? It was a bit of a scary thought. But incredibly exciting, too, because, well, what if it ran in the family? Sofie had said Danny didn't want to do magic as though everyone knew he *could*. So he must have inherited it from Uncle Jack, right?

"Sofie . . . do you know anything about my dad?"

Sofie concentrated very hard on licking chocolate off her whiskers.

"Because Uncle Jack said something the other day, and I wondered . . ."

"Lottie, I am sorry. I never met your father. Shall we go?" Sofie asked, jumping lightly from her chair. "I wish to sleep now. I am feeling emotionally delicate."

"You want to sleep because you ate a whole piece of chocolate gateau," Lottie muttered under her breath. Sofie's tummy was definitely nearer the ground than usual, and she was waddling slightly.

They walked slowly back to the shop, enjoying the sun, but the thoughts were still whirring at the back of Lottie's mind.

A couple of streets away, Lottie saw Zara and her friends gathered on the other side of the road, looking at something.

"Look!" she hissed discreetly to Sofie.

Sofie growled, low in her throat. "I would like to bite that Zara," she muttered. Obviously she was still feeling snappish from the fight with Selina.

Lottie nodded. "I know. Me too. Well, not bite, but you know what I mean. What are they doing anyway?" she added, as she saw Zara poke something with her foot.

Sofie peered across the road, and sniffed. "Something over there is scared, Lottie," she said at last. "I do not like those girls, not at all."

Lottie looked around. At least they weren't on a quiet street like the last time she'd had a showdown with Zara. There were people around, even though no one else had noticed what the girls were doing.

A frantic meow from inside the group of girls made Lottie stop wavering. Her sudden surge of anger at Zara's cruelty simply blocked out her fear.

"It's a cat, Sofie, and they're hurting it. How can they be so mean!" Lottie stomped across the road, and pushed one of Zara's friends out of the way.

The cat was cowering back against the wall, a poor, half-starved, scrawny-looking thing. Lottie picked it up quickly, and gave Zara a furious look. "How dare you? Were you kicking it?" she demanded.

"What's it got to do with you, *Lottie*?" Zara laughed, a high, angry laugh, but Lottie thought she sounded slightly ashamed. The rest of the girls were looking confused, and a couple of them were backing away slightly, as though they didn't want to be involved. Lottie looked around at them disgustedly, and started to walk away, carrying the cat, who seemed frozen in her arms.

"Where do you think you're going?" snapped Zara, grabbing at her. She could see her friends melting away, and she was trying to stay in control.

"Get off me!" Lottie yelled, and Sofie growled.

People in the street were starting to turn and look, and Zara decided on a tactical retreat. But not without one last attack. "Stupid sausage dog," she snarled, aiming a kick at Sofie.

Lottie gasped in horror, but Sofie was lightning fast when she needed to be. She pounced, with a strange twisting leap, and sank her teeth into Zara's flounced skirt, ripping it almost in half. Then she raced off, hissing to Lottie, who was watching in amazement, "Come on, *imbécile*!"

Several turns later, they paused for breath, Zara's shrieks still ringing in their ears.

"Is that fluffy little *thing* all right?" Sofie asked, peering up at the cat a little contemptuously.

Lottie looked at the cat carefully. It was lying limply in her arms. She wondered if it was in shock. "I'm not sure," she told Sofie, who growled rude-sounding French words under her breath, cursing Zara and the rest. Lottie couldn't see any obvious injuries, but she wanted Uncle Jack to have a look.

As they pushed open the pet shop door, the eerie hush gave Lottie a moment of uncertainty. Should she not have brought the cat here? It wasn't a magical creature, just a scruffy little stray. She looked around worriedly, realizing that in every cage, the animals had crowded forward and were watching with interest.

Uncle Jack and Horace looked up from the paper. The four black kittens were sitting on the counter with them. Obviously Uncle Jack had given in to their whining and let them out to explore. The mice were all looking decidedly jumpy, Lottie noticed.

"What is *that*?" Selina asked disgustedly, looking at the dirty pile of fur in Lottie's arms.

"Time for you lot to go back in your pen, I think," Uncle Jack said, casting a thoughtful look at Lottie. He grabbed an armful of cats and strode into the next room, dumping them unceremoniously into their pen to a chorus of yowls and delighted cheering from the mouse cages. He came back, looking interested.

Lottie cuddled the cat to her, suddenly feeling protective as Uncle Jack peered at her curiously over his glasses. "I know it's not magical," she burst out, "but we couldn't just leave it, they were going to hurt it, and —"

"Hey, hey, Lottie, slow down. You can tell me what happened in a minute." Uncle Jack gently took the cat, cradling it in his arms for a moment before laying it on the counter. It blinked at him nervously. "Poor little girl," he murmured, stroking under her chin, and the cat gave him a grateful look.

"She's a she?" Lottie asked.

"Mmm." Uncle Jack wasn't really listening. He was too busy running his hands gently over the cat, feeling for wounds. Lottie had noticed before that he seemed to have a magic touch, and even the grumpiest animals would relax when he stroked them. The cat actually managed a very small purr. Uncle Jack pursed his lips thoughtfully. "She's been in a few fights, I think. Some old scratches, here. I don't think she's been badly hurt today, though she seems terrified. Where did you say you found her?" he asked, suddenly turning his attention back to Lottie.

"That same group of girls that chased me and Sofie last week. We saw them on our way home. Zara, she's the worst one, she was kicking her."

Sofie coughed delicately.

"Oh yes!" Lottie looked lovingly down at her, and then gave Uncle Jack a stern glare. "You're not to tell Sofie off, Uncle Jack. We grabbed the cat, and then Zara tried to snatch her back, and she nearly kicked Sofie, so Sofie bit her, and tore her skirt. Just a little. She had to, honestly!"

There was a disbelieving snort from one of the pink mice, and Uncle Jack gave Sofie a *look*. "And I bet that was a hardship," he muttered. "But, Lottie, it was those same girls, you're sure? Are you all right?"

Lottie shrugged. "They *are* really scary," she admitted. "But I couldn't just leave them to it, could I? They might have really hurt her!"

Uncle Jack looked sadly down at the cat. "I don't understand people sometimes. I mean, she may be a stray and not much to look at, but that doesn't mean she's fair game."

"I think she's quite pretty actually," Lottie said defensively. "She's just thin, and a bit dirty." She gazed hopefully at the cat, searching for something to make Uncle Jack like her. "She's got the most enormous eyes, look!"

Uncle Jack didn't answer, and Lottie stared at him sadly. "I'm sorry, I shouldn't have brought her here, should I?"

"Why not?" Uncle Jack asked, sounding surprised. "What else would you do with her?" He was fetching a bowl and some food, and the cat seemed to perk up a little.

"But she's all scruffy, and, well, *normal*. You only have magical animals here. She doesn't fit in."

"We'd rather have her than Selina any day!" yelled a mouse, and there was a disgusted hissing noise from the kitten pen.

Uncle Jack laughed. "Just because she needs a bath, it doesn't mean she's not special, Lottie. She might turn into a beauty when she's not so scruffy. She's only a kitten still, really. She's got time to grow." He hesitated.

"Lottie . . . it doesn't always work like that anyway. There isn't a line between people who have magic and people who don't. Sometimes you just need to look deep down." He looked at the cat, now wolfing the bowl of food as though she thought it might sprout legs and run away if she wasn't quick. "Although the hidden depths would have to be quite hidden with this one. . . ."

8

"Ow!" Lottie gave the new cat a reproachful look and sucked her hand. "Hey, I rescued you, you can't bite me!"

The cat glared back, and Uncle Jack grinned. "Cats aren't known for being grateful, Lottie. And they *hate* baths."

Lottie stared at him angrily. "So why am I doing it and not you?"

Uncle Jack just grinned even more. "Well, like you said, you rescued her. . . ."

"But you're the one with the magic."

"Uh-huh. Enough magic to know not to try and bathe a cat. Here's the cat shampoo, Lottie dear." Uncle Jack waved a green glass bottle.

"I'm holding her still with both hands, you'll have to do it," Lottie said firmly. She was standing on a step in front of the big, old kitchen sink, up to her elbows in water, and covered in scratches. The cat *was* in the water, but she was poised to leap out as soon as Lottie loosened her grip.

Half the mice in the shop were lined up along the

kitchen windowsill among the geraniums, bouncing up and down and sniggering. The cat kept giving them filthy looks, but she was mostly distracted by the awfulness of being wet.

Uncle Jack trickled a stream of greeny liquid from the bottle onto the cat's fur. It smelled horrible, like lice shampoo. "Uuurgh, what's *in* that?" Lottie asked, wrinkling her nose. The cat breathed in and looked like she was going to keel over.

The mouse crowd all pretended to faint into each other's arms, squeaking in horror.

"Shut up, you guys! And don't moan, Lottie, it's good stuff. We might actually get to see what color she is under all that dirt." Uncle Jack helpfully rubbed the shampoo in, and poured a few jugfuls of water over the cat. She looked skinnier than ever, shivering and spiky-furred. But after she'd been rubbed dry with Danny's precious soccer-team bath towel, which Lottie noticed *after* Uncle Jack had swathed the spitting armful in it, the cat looked a lot better. Uncle Jack vanished into the shop and came back with another green glass bottle and a large spoon. The cat looked decidedly suspicious, and when Uncle Jack poured a spoonful of thick brown liquid, she attempted to escape out of the kitchen window, leaving Lottie with another set of scratches, and all the mice *in* the geraniums, hyperventilating, and cursing Lottie for nearly letting go.

"Mr. Murgatroyd's Patent Coat Restorer," Uncle Jack explained. "Fabulous stuff." He waved the bottle at Lottie, showing her the old-fashioned label with a glossy-furred cat in a huge blue bow. "Quentin Murgatroyd ran this shop before I did. Wonderful man, cats were his speciality. This tonic is still made to his secret recipe." Suddenly he swooped on the cat, who had foolishly been distracted by the way he was waving the bottle about, and poured the spoonful down her throat. The mice cheered, and nothing happened for about ten seconds, except that the cat's eyes grew wider and wider, as Lottie watched worriedly. Then she gave three enormous coughs, her eyes bugging out wildly, and blew a tiny stream of smoke from each nostril. She blinked dazedly, shook her head, and then looked at the spoon. "Mrowl?" she inquired hopefully.

"Sorry." Uncle Jack shook his head, screwing the top back on tightly. "Quentin always gave me dire warnings about overdosing. You might end up with whiskers down to your knees."

Lottie wasn't sure if it was Mr. Murgatroyd's tonic, or just the bath, but a few minutes later, when the cat had finally dried off, her fur looked thick and lustrous. She was still painfully thin, but she had a beautiful tabby-tortoiseshell coat, and with her huge green eyes, she was very striking.

The black kittens were less than impressed. They

were incredibly snobby, and they were horrified to be sharing their pen with what they called "a common tabby" (that was the politest thing they said) and one who couldn't even talk, much less do any magic.

Selina walked slowly all around the tabby cat, then sat down right in front of her, nose to nose, while her brothers watched, smirking. She looked like an Egyptian statue, some sort of cat goddess, and she knew it. The tabby cat shrank back, her ears laid low and her whiskers drooping. "How *interesting*," Selina purred. "Can it think at all, do we know?" She looked inquiringly at Lottie, her expression polite and curious.

"Stop it, Selina," Lottie snapped. "You know perfectly well she can."

"Actually, I know nothing about common cats," Selina said sweetly. "I've never met one."

Lottie sighed, and looked apologetically at the tabby. "It won't be for long, I promise."

"Good," Selina said, still staring haughtily at her new housemate. "We don't want to catch anything."

"I wasn't talking to you!"

"You don't think *that* understands, do you?" Selina asked disgustedly.

"Yes, I do, and so do you, or you wouldn't bother being so rude." Lottie resisted the urge to pull Selina's tail, but only just.

"She doesn't need to bother, it comes naturally," Midnight sniggered.

Uncle Jack spoiled his animals so much that the kittens' pen was enormous, with all sorts of tunnels and nests for them to play in. They didn't use the toys much, preferring to lounge about and bicker, but luckily it meant that the tabby cat could hide at the back of the pen out of the black kittens' way. They were too lazy to come and dig her out all the time, preferring just to make insulting remarks that they were fairly sure she could hear.

Lottie tried taking her out of the pen and stroking her, but she was terribly shy, and would only sit tensely against Lottie's shoulder. It took lots of petting to make her relax enough to purr, but that was hardly surprising after the fright she'd had. And now, after she'd been rescued, she was spending her whole time being bullied and jeered at. Lottie almost wondered if the little cat would be happier back out as a stray, even if it did mean people like Zara could chase her.

Lottie was sitting stroking the tabby cat on one of the chairs behind the counter, wondering how to cheer her up, but she couldn't ignore the hissing complaints coming from the kittens' pen in the next room. They hated Lottie paying so much attention to the new cat, and they kept up a constant stream of snarling whenever she cuddled her. Lottie knew the tabby cat could hear them too. Her shoulders were hunched, and her ears were flat against her head, even when Lottie tried to rub behind them.

"This is ridiculous," Lottie muttered. She got up, snuggling the tense body of the cat against her shoulder. Despite several enormous meals, she was still so thin that Lottie was sure she could count her bones. "We're going upstairs, all right?" she snapped at the black kittens, putting her head around the door.

There was a stunned silence. Lottie grinned to herself. This was the last thing they wanted — Lottie and the scruffy commoner upstairs where they couldn't even see what was going on. Lottie could almost hear them frantically trying to work out where they'd gone wrong.

The tabby cat seemed much more relaxed away from the poisonous comments downstairs. "So much for them not having any magic yet," Lottie muttered. "That had to be some kind of cat curse, even I feel better now."

The cat purred gratefully, and jumped onto Lottie's bed.

Lottie sat down next to her, and stroked her thoughtfully. "Maybe not, though. I suppose it's just the same as someone whispering about you at school." She shuddered, thinking about starting at Netherbridge Hill in September. She wondered miserably if she would be in the same class as Zara.

A small furry head inserted itself comfortingly under her hand. Then the cat climbed into Lottie's lap and stood up, lightly resting her paws on Lottie's shoulder, and rubbing the side of her face along her chin.

Lottie giggled, and gave the cat a very gentle hug. "You're good at cheering people up," she murmured — and the cat's green eyes flashed, but Lottie wasn't looking.

Uncle Jack was trying to find the cat a home, but he hadn't had any luck so far. He was very choosy about homes for his animals, and he said she needed an owner who would understand that she was shy and nervous.

Early one evening, a couple of days after she'd rescued the cat, Lottie was on a stepladder in a dark corner, cleaning out one of the mouse cages, when she heard footsteps in the kitchen. The white mice were all perched on the cage roof, pointing out bits that she'd missed, and arguing for an extra ration of sunflower seeds, so she looked around quickly to check who was visiting, and whether she should shush the mice.

A slender figure in black slipped around the door, and Lottie felt a jolt of excitement. Although Ariadne was at the shop most days, Lottie still found being around a real witch fascinating.

"Oooh, look, Ariadne's back," chirped one of the mice. "Has she decided on one of those kittens yet, Lottie?"

"I hope she takes that horrible, fat Midnight," put in another mouse, peering down. "He keeps looking at me and licking his chops."

"You go and talk to her, Lottie, try and get her to take them all," the first mouse suggested. "Sooner they're sold, the better. Urgh." He shuddered. "They give me the creeps."

"We'll get ourselves back in the cage, don't worry. Just stick a bit of fresh bedding down. Lovely. There you go. Go on, get rid of the little monsters for us!"

Lottie was giggling as she climbed down the ladder. She still found it funny being bossed around by mice. Especially with their tiny, squeaky voices.

Uncle Jack, Danny, and Ariadne were already gazing down into the kittens' pen, while they purred and preened before her. Sofie joined Lottie, shaking her head disgustedly. "Little fiends," she muttered to Lottie. "I pity that witch."

"I know," Lottie murmured, her eyes fixed hungrily on Ariadne. She found the witch scarily fascinating. Ariadne seemed to be wearing a black fur scarf, even though it was another sweltering day. Lottie was just wondering if witches always felt cold when the scarf spoke.

"What do you want, child?" it snapped at her grumpily.

Lottie gulped. Had Ariadne bewitched an old fur so that it could talk? She shuddered. The scarf had milky green eyes, glowing like opals, and it was staring right at her.

"Cat got your tongue?" chuckled the scarf, winking at Sofie, and obviously thinking itself very funny. Lottie suddenly caught on.

"Oh! You're Shadow! I thought you were . . ." she stopped, not sure if Shadow might be insulted that she'd mistaken him for a fur scarf.

Ariadne was smiling around at her. Lottie wished she didn't always behave like a silly child, crying and saying stupid things, when the witch turned up. Ariadne just seemed to have that effect on her.

"Camouflage. Very useful skill. If I put my paws in my mouth, you'd swear I was stuffed." Shadow stood up on Ariadne's shoulders to look at Lottie better. She realized that his eyes were glassy-looking because he was going blind. "So which of this group do you think we should buy?"

Lottie opened her mouth and shut it again help-lessly. Sofie and Danny were watching her and grinning, and she scowled at them. The kittens were so irritating that she didn't really want to saddle Ariadne with any of them, but then, she had a feeling Shadow might have been a pretty horrible kitten himself.

"They're all very clever," she said, trying to be tact-ful, and very conscious of four pairs of emerald green eyes burning into her.

"And you can't stand them. Well, that's interesting." Shadow curled back around Ariadne's neck and gazed down at the kittens, who glared back furiously.

Ariadne stroked his head gently, and sighed. "We have to choose, Shadow. You know I'm not doing this because I want to."

Shadow made a noise that was half growl, half purr, and jumped down, landing perfectly, despite his age. Now that Lottie looked closely, she could see that his muzzle was silvered, but he was still beautiful.

Shadow stared thoughtfully into the pen, his whiskers flickering as he examined the kittens. "I can't tell any difference," he declared haughtily at last. "Just have the biggest." He strolled off, his head and tail held very high. He looked as though he was examining the lizards, but somehow Lottie didn't think he was really seeing them.

Ariadne gazed helplessly after him, her eyes shining with tears. Then she turned back to the pen, her shoulders slumping slightly. "I so hoped it would help, bringing him," she murmured to Lottie, Danny, and Uncle Jack. "I didn't want to come back with a new kitten and have them hate each other."

Uncle Jack patted her awkwardly on the shoulder. "He'll get used to it. Hopefully when you start training the new one, he won't be able to resist getting involved. He's too bossy not to!"

Ariadne nodded. "I hope so." She knelt down in front of the kittens. "So, which of you is it to be?" She stared at them, looking deep into their eyes, and they stopped their jostling and gazed back at her — it was as though she had hypnotized them.

"Stop!"

Everyone jumped. Ariadne's connection with the kittens was broken, and they hissed and spat angrily. Midnight's tail was sticking out like a brush, and Selina started to wash furiously — they could feel that Ariadne had been staring into their minds, and they didn't like it.

Shadow walked quickly around to the front of the pen. "There's another cat here, hiding. I can feel her. You must make her come out. She won't listen to me."

"Her! She doesn't understand what you're trying to say to her, she's just a dumb stray Lottie picked up," Selina said disgustedly, licking her paw and swiping at her ears.

Shadow ignored her. "You must see her," he told Ariadne urgently. "She's very strong, she can cloak herself almost completely. I nearly missed her."

Danny passed Lottie a handful of cat treats from behind the counter, and she went around to the back of the pen. The tabby cat had been hungry for so long that food almost always worked as a bribe. Lottie shook the treats invitingly, and a set of black and white whiskers appeared twitchily from inside an old cardboard box. A pink nose pushed the flaps out of the way, and a pair of stripy paws followed. The little cat scrambled out and landed with a thump. Lottie sprinkled a trail around to the front, and the cat followed it, munching daintily. She reached the last cat treat, then looked up to find Ariadne, and Shadow, staring raptly at her. Her big green eyes widened to shocked circles, and she stared back, caught.

At last Ariadne sighed and looked up. The little cat was shaking her head dazedly, her eyes still fixed on the witch, no longer shocked but full of a deep contentment. "Why didn't you tell me about her?" Ariadne breathed delightedly.

"I didn't even think about it." Uncle Jack was shaking his head. "We've only had her a couple of days. Are you sure?"

"She can cloak *almost* as well as me," Shadow said proudly. "We'll have this one," he told Uncle Jack loftily.

"You can't!" Midnight meowed, looking horror-struck. "She isn't black."

"She has stripes, she's a *common tabby*," Selina hissed. "An alley cat."

"Oh, be quiet," Shadow said disgustedly. "Come here, child." He went right up to the pen, and pressed his nose against the wire.

Trembling, the tabby cat crept forward, her tummy to the ground. The happiness had vanished from her eyes as she heard Midnight's and Selina's taunts. She didn't dare disobey Shadow, but now her whiskers drooped miserably again. At last, she was nose to nose with him.

Lottie couldn't really see what Shadow did — it seemed as though he simply breathed on her — but her laid-back ears twitched, and she raised her glowing eyes to stare lovingly at him, and at Ariadne.

"She's called Tabitha," Shadow said, with a sort of fatherly pride.

Lottie could hardly bear to say it, but she had to. "You do know — I mean, Midnight is right, she's not a magical cat." Ariadne and Shadow were looking at her in surprise, and she added miserably, in a whisper, "She can't *talk*." It was so unfair. The most perfect, wonderful new owner for the poor cat, and she wouldn't want her after all.

Ariadne laughed, a low chuckle that made Tabitha purr delightedly. She reached down, opened the pen, and picked her up, snuggling the thin body against her shoulder. "Oh, Lottie. It's all right." She scratched behind Tabitha's ears, smiling as the purr deepened to an ecstatic rumble. "We can teach her."

Shadow rubbed his head against Lottie's leg, and then wove himself happily around Ariadne. "Bright girl like that, she'll pick it up." He glanced contemptuously at the black kittens, who were watching Tabitha and Ariadne with slitted eyes. "We can make sure we teach her manners at the same time."

Uncle Jack gave a huge sigh, but he was smiling. "Well, that's a sale lost. Tabitha isn't mine to sell. If she's happy to go with you, she's yours. I don't suppose you need a basket?"

Ariadne smiled and shook her head. "It wouldn't fit on. Shadow will show her what to do."

Uncle Jack nodded, and Lottie watched in surprise as Ariadne walked through the back of the shop out to the yard.

"Where are they going?" she muttered to Danny, and he grinned at her. "Watch."

"Come on, Lottie." Sofie was trotting out, too, her tail swishing excitedly. "I love to see them do this."

An old broom that Lottie hadn't noticed before was propped up in the corner of the yard. It looked dusty and cobwebbed, as though it had been there for years, but Lottie was sure it hadn't. Her heart began to bump painfully against her ribs as she watched Ariadne pick it up. Was she really about to see someone fly on a broomstick?

Sofie was watching wistfully as Shadow showed Tabitha how to grip the twigs with her claws. Ariadne pulled her skirt in close and sat gracefully sideways on the broom. She murmured something, and the broom shuddered.

"Ahhh," Sofie sighed enviously as Ariadne and the two cats floated into the air.

"Won't someone see?" Lottie whispered, gazing into the sky.

"Not unless they're *really* looking," Uncle Jack said, smiling. "Ariadne is like Tabitha, she's very good at not being seen." He waved as the broom sped higher, and Ariadne waved back. The cats looked down rather smugly at the little group below, and Lottie was almost sure she heard a soft, shy voice call, "Good-bye! And thank you!"

The broomstick looked more like a bird now, a black speck gliding on the wind, and at last it disappeared altogether. At last Lottie stopped trying to see them any more, her eyes burning with the effort. She took a deep shuddering gasp of air, feeling as if she might have forgotten to breathe for the last few minutes, and looked around at her uncle and Danny.

Uncle Jack was smiling. "You never forget the first time you see it." He put his arm around Lottie, and she leaned against him, trembling.

Sofie looked thoughtfully at Lottie, and then up at Uncle Jack, a curious expression in her dark eyes.

He nodded slightly, a smile lifting the corner of his mouth as he looked down at Lottie's glowing face and dreamy eyes. It was time Lottie knew.

After all, you could never tell from looking what a person was like inside.

9

"Lottie, you're not busy this evening, are you?" Uncle Jack asked, putting his head around the kitchen door as Lottie did the dishes after lunch the next day.

Lottie gave him a surprised look. All she ever did in the evenings was watch TV, sometimes e-mail Hannah and Rachel, and pretend she wasn't waiting for her mum to call.

Uncle Jack seemed to see what she meant. "No, well, good," he muttered. "Family dinner. Ariadne's coming too. Wants us all to be there." He disappeared, *almost* literally.

Lottie gazed thoughtfully after him. She wondered if he had an announcement to make. Were he and Ariadne going to get married? It would be fantastic if Ariadne lived at the shop, too, Lottie thought dreamily. She could ask her things all the time, and Ariadne might let her watch . . . well, Lottie wasn't at all sure what exactly, because she had no idea what Ariadne actually *did*. She shook her head, feeling silly.

Ariadne brought Shadow and Tabitha with her that evening, and Lottie was amazed by how different

Tabitha looked already. She was still thin, but she seemed graceful, and so happy. Her whiskers almost glittered, and her eyes were a deep, luminous green. Ariadne and Shadow were clearly very proud of her. The two cats sat on Ariadne's lap, and ate most of her dinner. Sofie sat on her cushions on the other side of the table, stiff with disapproval. She might have helped to rescue Tabitha, but it didn't mean she wanted cats in her kitchen all the time.

Even with Sofie glaring, it was a lovely meal. Uncle Jack was a very good cook, and he'd made a real effort. He'd had a huge pile of stained old cookbooks on the counter all afternoon, and kept stepping out to the kitchen to check the contents of cabinets. "Do you like mushrooms?" he'd asked Lottie anxiously, popping up under the ladder just as she was refilling the mice's water bottles, and nearly making her fall off. He was clutching a handful of purple fungus.

"That's a toadstool!" one of the pink mice yelled.

"Don't eat it! Don't eat it!" And they all started running around and around their cage, shrieking dire warnings at Lottie. "It's poisonous! Fatal! You're all going to die!"

Septimus the black rat peered thoughtfully out of his cage. "Of course it isn't poisonous," he said wearily. "But it will taste absolutely disgusting," he added to Uncle Jack. "Stop trying to be fancy, and use organic ones, for goodness' sake."

Lottie grinned, remembering Septimus's beady glare. "I just liked the color," Uncle Jack had murmured apologetically as he headed back to the kitchen.

Eventually they stacked a tower of plates next to the sink, and Uncle Jack set his battered silver coffeepot on the table, with a big plate of lemon bars. Lottie had just gotten herself nicely covered in sugar, when Uncle Jack cleared his throat.

The two cats, who weren't keen on chocolate mousse and had snoozed through dessert, suddenly sat bolt upright, and Sofie stopped trying to sneak another lemon bar.

Lottie looked around, feeling suddenly nervous. They were all staring at her.

"What is it?" she asked worriedly.

Uncle Jack smiled at her. "We've got something to show you," he said gently. He passed her a book, quite an old one, with a leather cover, and for a moment Lottie was sure it was full of amazing spells. She was almost disappointed to see that it was a photo album.

"Open it," Danny said. He sounded strangely excited, and Lottie undid the ribbon that held the cover together.

The first page was obviously Uncle Jack's wedding photo. It was the first picture Lottie had seen of Danny's mum; he looked very like her. But Lottie could sense that this wasn't what everyone was waiting for her to see. She worked her way through a couple more pages, mostly baby photos of Danny, then gasped as she turned over another page. Her dad!

"I've never seen this picture," she murmured, very gently tracing the line of his face with her finger.

"Look closer, Lottie," her uncle said gently.

Lottie peered at the photo, at last taking in the background. "But . . . that's here. My dad's *here*," she muttered stupidly. She looked up at her uncle, and then around at the others. They were all watching her. Lottie flipped through a few more pages, and then stared at Uncle Jack. "And this one's me."

Her uncle nodded.

"I've been here before?"

"Lottie," her uncle said gently. "Lottie, you lived here."

Lottie lay on her bed, in that pink-and-white room that had seemed so strangely familiar, her head almost aching with secrets unfolded. Uncle Jack had let her take the album upstairs, and she was gazing hungrily at the pictures of herself and her mum and dad here at the shop.

There were ones of Lottie and Danny, too, and her with Simona, Danny's mum. Lottie was fighting to remember any of the moments in the pictures, because they all looked so happy, but she couldn't. It felt so unfair.

Actually, Lottie realized, looking at the photos again, her mum *didn't* look all that happy. She looked uncomfortable, and somehow lonely. As though she'd been left out of something.

"We tried, Lottie," Uncle Jack had explained, clearly finding it difficult. "Your mum's a wonderful person, and we all loved her. But — she just wasn't happy here. She couldn't see it, what was truly going on, and it made things so hard for her. It was hard on your dad, too, loving her so much, and having to hide half his life from her."

"But why couldn't she see?" Lottie asked, not really understanding.

"Some people just can't," Ariadne put in gently. "It can be partly that they don't want to. Or that they just have too much else on their minds."

"After your dad died, there was nothing tying her to the shop. We would have loved her to stay, but she'd never settled here." Uncle Jack sighed. "I've always felt guilty about that. That was why I was so glad when she called." He smiled at Lottie. "And I was curious about you. You look just like him, you know. Tom, your dad."

Staring at the photos now, Lottie could see that it was true. She'd only ever seen a couple of pictures before. It was as though her mum had tried to forget that part of their lives. But now Lottie was back, and she couldn't help thinking, if she looked so much like her dad, did that mean she was like him in other ways too?

Had she inherited the magic?

Lottie's bedroom door squeaked, and she jumped. Tabitha squeezed apologetically into the room, and stopped, one paw held up hesitantly as though she wasn't sure if she was welcome.

"Hey, Tabitha." Lottie made kiss-kiss noises to her, and patted the bed, and she leaped up, curling firmly between Lottie and the photo album, nosing it shut.

"Yeah, I know. You're probably right," Lottie sighed. "I've stared at it for long enough already." She gazed into Tabitha's green eyes, and felt herself relax a little. "I wish you could talk," she murmured. "I know Shadow said you would when you were ready, it's just that I feel like you might understand. This whole magic thing's been dropped on us both. It would be really nice to have someone to talk to about it."

Tabitha licked Lottie's chin sympathetically.

"I know it's not the same, but you could talk to me," said a voice.

This time Lottie nearly fell off the bed. Ariadne was sitting on her windowsill, her hands cradling two of the pink mice, who now seemed to be spending more time in Lottie's room than their own cage.

"How did you *do* that?" Lottie squawked, wondering for a horrified moment if Ariadne could turn into a bat and fly in through windows. Or was that vampires?

"It's because Tabitha's here," Ariadne explained. "We're bonded, and she makes me stronger. She called me."

"Oh . . ."

"Lottie, she knew that you needed someone. I think you need to talk too. You must have loads of questions." Ariadne curled up on the bed next to her, and they stroked Tabitha together, making the little cat squirm with delight. The mice retreated to the top of Ariadne's head, to be as far away from Tabitha as possible.

Lottie sighed. "So many that I can't think what to ask first . . ." She looked up at Ariadne, knowing that the witch could probably read her mind if she wanted to. That would make things simpler. Lottie grinned. Somehow, admitting how powerful Ariadne was made her relax a little. Whatever she said, she was going to sound stupid, so she might as well go straight for the big question. "Ariadne, I know Uncle Jack said that anyone could have magic in them, but it does run in families, too, doesn't it?"

Ariadne nodded.

"Uncle Jack is, my dad was — but I know my mum's about as unmagical as you can get — do you think I might be able to — to do anything?"

Lottie stared anxiously at Ariadne. What if she said there was no chance, that Lottie was just like her mum? But Ariadne smiled at her. "Do you remember the first time we met, Lottie? I tried to spell you. It was rude of me, actually, but I was anxious about seeing the kittens, and I just did it without thinking. You threw me out and closed your mind to me, Lottie. The first person who's managed that in years. I have no idea exactly what your powers will be, but they're there. There's no question."

"Oh." Lottie found that a small, foolish smile had appeared on her face and stuck. She couldn't think of anything else to say.

One of the pink mice leaned down precariously. "And don't forget, Lottie, you could always tell we weren't just normal mice. You knew there was something special about us. You noticed how *terribly* magical we are!"

"I'll teach you, if you like," Ariadne added, almost hesitantly. "I'd enjoy it. I've never had an apprentice, and the witch who taught me said she learned more teaching someone else than she ever did being taught herself."

"Would I be an apprentice *witch*?" Lottie asked.

Ariadne shrugged. "I think you're whatever you want to be. You don't have to call it anything. You're doing this to learn what you *could* be."

Lottie nodded, an absurd happiness welling up inside her. Right now, she felt as though she could be anything she wanted.

10

The happiness wore off. It wasn't that Lottie had expected magic to be easy, she just hadn't expected it to be *impossible*.

At Ariadne's apartment the day after the family dinner, Lottie couldn't help looking around for cauldrons, and stuffed alligators and things, but it wasn't that sort of place at all. It was all painted in pale, fresh colors, and there were big vases of strongly scented flowers everywhere. A huge mirror was hanging in the middle of the living room wall, so that you saw it as soon as you walked in. It made Lottie stop short. The glass was slightly misty, and mottled around the edges, and the frame was made of dark wood, twisted and carved into all sorts of figures and patterns. Lottie felt as though she could look at it, and into it, forever. Tabitha butted her head gently into Lottie's leg, and Lottie broke the gaze of her reflection in the deceptive glass, and shivered. She couldn't help thinking of the mirror in *Snow White*, and she wondered if Ariadne talked to hers. She and Hannah and Rachel had almost worn out her copy of the Disney DVD, they'd watched it so often. Lottie wished she could tell them what she was doing now.

But apart from the mirror, the most magical-looking thing she could see was a highly complicated coffee machine. Lottie smiled nervously at Ariadne. "You should have Sofie over," she suggested, glad to have something to talk about.

Ariadne grinned back. "Most people don't appreciate what magical stuff coffee is." She sounded dead serious, but Lottie wasn't sure.

Disappointingly, Ariadne didn't chant any long, complicated spells, or even draw a circle of protection. Lots of the Web sites Lottie had looked up on Uncle Jack's computer had suggested that was a vital first step. All she did was light a very boring white candle (which came out of a box that she kept under the sink next to the paper towels) and drip some wax to stick it to a saucer. Tabitha and Shadow jumped up onto the table and sat next to Ariadne. Then they all stared at it. For an awfully long time.

Lottie wasn't really sure what she was supposed to see, and after a while, she said so.

"I don't know," Ariadne admitted. "These things are different for everyone. To be honest, you don't really need the candle, but it's useful to have something to look at, to help clear your mind."

Ten minutes later, Ariadne blew the candle out, and Lottie sighed, half relieved, half disappointed.

"Don't worry. It might take a while to get the hang of it," Ariadne said reassuringly, but that didn't make Lottie feel much better. "It wasn't what you expected, was it?" Ariadne asked, her voice sympathetic, but a little amused, and Lottie felt silly.

"I don't know what I thought it would be like," she murmured. Then she shrugged. "I don't even know what you *do*! You're a witch, but what does that mean? What do you actually do all day?"

"Drink coffee," Shadow muttered, stretching out his paws and yawning.

Ariadne scratched him under the chin. "People ask me to do things, Lottie. Most of the time I try to persuade them that what they think they want to do isn't what they *actually* want to do, or even if it is, they shouldn't . . . I suppose the simplest way to put it is that I help people to do the right thing — but that can be quite complicated."

"Do you ever do anything . . ." Lottie wasn't quite sure how to ask, but she couldn't help thinking of that mirror, and Snow White's evil stepmother.

Shadow chuckled, a low, throaty noise, his misty eyes fixed on Lottie. "She wants to know if we dabble in the Black Arts."

Lottie nodded, her heart suddenly thudding.

Ariadne stood up and started to fiddle with the coffee machine, pouring milk and adjusting dials and buttons. But it was shiny and silver, and Lottie could see her face in it, serious, frowning slightly.

Shadow's hazy eyes were still fastened on Lottie, and she had the strangest feeling that Ariadne didn't need to be looking at her if he was. Lottie darted a glance at Tabitha, too — and the little cat's huge, lamplike green eyes locked on to hers, pulling her in, and making her gasp.

"No!" she squeaked, jumping up.

Ariadne turned and looked at her, her eyes as green as Tabitha's, with something of the same eerie glow. "How black is black, Lottie?" she asked gently. "Tabitha and Shadow and I just tried to see inside your mind. Don't you think that might be the worst thing you could ever do to anyone? To see everything, all their wishes and dreams and fears, and leave them nothing that's just their own? Imagine reading your best friend's diary, and knowing all her secrets — if we went into someone's mind, Lottie, we'd know the secrets they even keep from themselves."

"What did you see?" Lottie said, half-sobbing, her nails digging so far into her palms that they were almost cutting.

Shadow's growly chuckle sounded sinister this time, and Lottie could suddenly see why some people were afraid of cats. But his voice was gentle and purring when he answered her. "Nothing, Lottie."

Tabitha walked across the table and rubbed her head gently across Lottie's arm. All at once the air in the kitchen seemed clearer again, and Lottie's thudding heart slowed down. She slid back onto her chair, her legs still shaking.

"You were linked up with Shadow and Tabitha," she said slowly. "Like yesterday, when you said that you were bonded. I wanted to ask you what that meant."

Ariadne brought a cup of coffee to the table, rich steam curling off it and making Lottie see strange patterns in the air. Ariadne sipped slowly, her eyes dark and catlike now through the steam. "They're my familiars, Lottie," she explained. "Some witches have them. They make me stronger. If we want, we can weave ourselves together. Like just now — I could see you because Shadow and Tabitha could. You understand now why it was so important to find the right cat."

Lottie nodded. "Why did you try to get in my head?" she asked suddenly.

"To see what would happen." Ariadne stared at her thoughtfully. "You guard yourself very carefully, Lottie."

"I'm not trying to," Lottie admitted. "I didn't do it on purpose, it just happened."

"Well, that's what we're trying to find," Ariadne said. "Once you know where your power is, then you can use it." She handed Lottie the candle. "Homework. Just keep looking."

It was only when Lottie got back to the shop that she realized that Ariadne hadn't really answered her question.

Staring at a candle did not get any easier. Lottie practiced the next day while she was minding the shop, sitting at the counter with her chin on her folded arms, gazing into the purple heart of the flame.

So far she had fallen asleep twice, but not much else had happened.

"What are you doing?"

Lottie jumped. She'd been dozing off again, and Danny had come downstairs without her noticing. She flushed pink.

"You nearly set your hair on fire." Danny was grinning.

Lottie sat up straight and tried to look dignified. "I was doing something Ariadne showed me," she said firmly.

"It's a sleeping spell, isn't it, Lottie?" Selina called from the kittens' pen in the next room. "It's working *so* well!" And all four black kittens meowed with laughter.

Danny clicked his fingers, and the flame flickered

out at once. "For your own safety, Lottie," he said, his grin changing to a smirk.

Lottie stared at him, shocked. She hadn't known he could do anything like that. "You — you . . ."

"Just because I *don't* usually, doesn't mean I *can't*!" Danny shrugged. "More bother than it's worth most of the time."

"But how did you . . . ?" Lottie wailed. "And how come you can and I can't?!"

Danny looked vague. "I don't know. You just do it. Look inside yourself and it's there, I suppose." He strolled out of the shop door, leaving Lottie feeling useless.

Later that afternoon, Uncle Jack shooed Lottie out of the shop, telling her to get some fresh air, she looked exhausted. Lottie suddenly realized that she'd hardly seen Sofie since the family dinner, and she hadn't talked over all this history with her at all. She went to find her to suggest a walk to the park, with maybe a coffee on the way home.

Lottie eventually found her in the storeroom, curled up on a bag of hay and unconvincingly asleep.

"Sofie!" Lottie tickled behind one ear.

Sofie just twitched irritably, and breathed out in the faintest suggestion of a growl.

"Sorry! I just wondered if you wanted to come for a walk," Lottie said, feeling hurt.

"No!" Sofie snapped back over her shoulder. "Ask Tabitha!"

"Sofie! That's so not fair. Anyway, cats don't go for walks."

"Speak to her nicely, and I'm sure she will." It was a muffled mutter as the little dog curled up on the sack again, very determinedly.

Lottie backed out of the storeroom, confused. Had she been neglecting Sofie for Tabitha? She supposed she had. But she hadn't meant to! It was just the way things had happened, and Tabitha was part of her time with Ariadne, and —

All right, so she had forgotten about Sofie until she wanted something from her. Miserably guilty, Lottie gave up on the walk idea, and went upstairs to lie on her bed, feeling lonely. It was only now that Sofie wouldn't talk to her that Lottie realized how important the grumpy dachshund's company was. She'd been relying on Sofie to have something useful to say about how hard she was finding Ariadne's task.

"Lottie, phone!" Uncle Jack was yelling up the stairs. Mum! It was bound to be. Lottie raced down to grab the phone, and sat on the stairs. Suddenly her mother's voice was incredibly welcome — she was so *normal*. It was a week since they'd spoken, and so much had happened that it seemed far longer.

"Hi, Mum!"

"You sound happier than when I last talked to you." Lottie's mum's voice was pleased, a little relieved.

She was feeling guilty about me, Lottie guessed. "Have you found out when you can come and visit?" she asked eagerly. In their last phone call, her mum had said she might be able to come back to England for a weekend.

"Oh, Lottie, I'm so sorry" — and she actually did sound sorry, Lottie thought dully — "it won't be for a while, I'm afraid. We're working on the weekends, too, it's just so busy here." She paused, feeling Lottie's disappointment. "Shall I send you some more of those chocolates? Did you like them?"

There was no point in arguing with her, Lottie knew. Her mum seemed to have this amazing ability to divide her life up into boxes, and tidy it all away. Right now, she was probably making a note on her computer — *Lottie, chocolates* — and that would be the Lottie box taped up again for a while.

"That would be nice," she said sadly, and quietly answered her mum's polite questions about Uncle Jack and Danny and the shop. Her mum promised again to try to find some time to get away and see her, but Lottie knew it wouldn't happen.

"You could come and see me!" her mum said brightly. "Not this weekend, of course, and I'm not sure about the next one, but soon . . . anyway, I must go, Lottie, I've got another call. Bye, darling!"

The phone made a dull buzzing noise as Lottie sat holding it. She felt so lonely, abandoned almost. She leaned against the wall and closed her eyes, very tired suddenly. Perhaps she could just go to sleep here for a while. After all, no one would miss me, she thought self-pityingly, almost enjoying being as miserable as possible.

The soft brush of fur against her leg wasn't a surprise. Tabitha seemed to have an amazing ability to turn up when she was needed. Now that Lottie thought about it, she could hear Ariadne, too, in the shop chatting to Uncle Jack.

Lottie stroked behind her soft brown ears. "You know, Sofie's really annoyed with you," she murmured.

Tabitha's eyes closed gently. She didn't seem too worried.

"My mum's not going to come over," Lottie told her. "I should have known she didn't mean it. She really likes it over there without me, I think. She keeps saying it's because she's so busy at work, but I reckon she's just glad to have gotten rid of me." Lottie's voice wobbled. "Sometimes I don't think she actually loves me very much."

"Prrrp!" Tabitha sounded shocked.

"Well, she doesn't want to be with me, does she?"

Tabitha's eyes glowed like emeralds in the dark of the stairway. "People show love in different ways, Lottie." The voice was soft and warm, with just a hint of a purr.

"You heard what Uncle Jack said about her not liking the shop. Maybe I remind her of being here, and Dad, and everything. . . ." Lottie faltered to a stop. "You actually said that, didn't you?" she whispered. "You spoke?"

Tabitha gave her the smuggest of cat looks. "Shadow taught me very well, I think. I like talking. You're the first person I've tried it with."

Lottie hugged her, forgetting to be miserable. "You're so clever! Oh, Tabitha, you star."

"It just shows, you can learn anything if you try, Lottie. The magic will come for you too."

Lottie nodded. "I suppose you're right." She stared at Tabitha's whiskers, so as not to have to look into those deep green, truthful eyes. "Tabitha, do you think when it does . . . do you think it will be even harder with Mum? She doesn't want to be with me now, and if I change, become all magical like Dad . . ."

Tabitha brushed her whiskers over Lottie's cheek, and purred in her ear. "Why should you change? You'll still be you. And I don't think you're being fair to your mother. I'm sure she loves you."

Lottie sighed. "It's so hard to talk to her over the phone. I wish I could see her."

Tabitha shrugged delicately. "So go."

"How?" Lottie laughed. "I don't have a broomstick, Tabitha."

Tabitha purred mysteriously. "Not yet. But, Lottie, your power is all there, even I can feel it. It makes my whiskers tingle. The magic will find a way."

12

It was all very well, Lottie thought grumpily, for Tabitha to say she'd find a way, but how? And more to the point, *when*?

"Lottie, I hate to say this, but are you really trying?" Ariadne asked, not angrily, but sounding tired. They seemed to have been at it for hours today. It was early evening, and they were all worn out.

Lottie sighed so heavily that the candle flame wavered and almost went out. "Yes! Honestly, I really am. I just don't seem to be able to do it. Maybe you've all made a mistake and I don't have any magic after all."

"Nonsense," Shadow snapped briskly. "Full of it. Just not making the effort."

"But I am!" Lottie began to protest, when Tabitha broke in. Her voice was soft and slightly hesitant, for she'd only been talking for two days, but still everyone listened to her.

"Lottie has too much else to worry about," she murmured. "She's upset about her mother being so distant, and also Sofie is still angry with her. She can't concentrate."

Ariadne sighed, stretched, and nodded, and blew the candle out herself. "Go on, Lottie. Go and sort it out with Sofie. Let's see if it makes a difference."

Lottie found Sofie sitting like a statue in front of the black kittens' pen. Her spine was rigid in the way it only was when she was furious; she looked as though she'd been carved out of jet. Lottie leaned in the doorway between the two rooms of the shop, wondering what to say. Sofie hadn't noticed her. She was transfixed by Selina and the others, who were coiling themselves around their cage like snakes, twisting in and out of each other in a mesmerizing ballet. Their voices twined around Sofie, and Lottie could feel them drawing her in too.

"Such a pity that Lottie doesn't want to spend her time with you anymore," Selina cooed.

Midnight brushed along the front of the cage, his back arching. "Does it make you angry, being abandoned for an alley cat?" he purred silkily.

"It should," Selina whispered. "You should fight back, Sofie darling. Chase her."

"Bite her!" hissed the others. "Tear her fur! Send her back where she came from!"

Sofie jumped to her feet suddenly, losing her eerie stillness. "No!" she barked sharply. "I am not listening!

I am not!" She spun around, saw Lottie, and gasped, her black eyes wide and haunted.

"Don't listen to them, Sofie!" Lottie swooped down and grabbed the little dog, her eyes full of tears. "They're wrong. Please don't listen!" She scooped Sofie into her arms, and raced upstairs to her room. Then she put Sofie gently down on her bed.

"I'm sorry, I shouldn't have grabbed you like that. But I had to get you away! I know Uncle Jack says they can't do spells, but they were bewitching you, they really were. They did it to Tabitha too!"

Sofie's whiskers were drooping. "They have no real power, Lottie. They can only hurt you if you listen to what they say. . . ." She laid her nose on her paws sadly.

"But you don't believe them, do you?" Lottie begged her. "It isn't true." Then she sighed and slid off the bed, kneeling on the floor to be face-to-face with Sofie. "It is — it is a little bit true, I suppose . . . not Tabitha making me ignore you, but suddenly finding out about all of it — my dad, and the lessons with Ariadne, and me maybe having magic in me too. I got carried away. But, Sofie, when you wouldn't talk to me yesterday, I realized how much I need you to be my friend. I really missed you, and I'm very, very sorry. Honestly."

Sofie sniffed, and looked at Lottie out of the corner of one eye. "Have you got any chocolate?" she demanded, with a return to her grand manner, but Lottie knew she was forgiven. She grabbed the latest box her mum had sent, and set about finding Sofie's favorite violet creams.

"Have Selina and Midnight and the others been saying that sort of stuff all the time?" Lottie asked a little later, through a mouthful of caramel.

Sofie nodded. "I tried not to listen," she said thickly, "but they get to you, those cats."

"I'm not surprised you didn't want to talk to me," Lottie muttered. "And they were trying to get you to fight Tabitha. That's just devious. They're using you because *they* hate her. I can't believe they're that sneaky!"

"Huh. Believe it. Selina, she is a she-devil." Sofie looked hopefully at the chocolate box, and gracefully accepted a truffle. "So, the magic is going well, then?" she asked gruffly, clearly trying not to sound too interested.

"Nope." Lottie picked the little chocolate shavings off the top of her orange cream, and shrugged. "I can't do whatever it is that Ariadne wants me to do to find my power. It's in me, they all say, but I have to unlock it. And I can't get at it. So, nothing's happening." She gave Sofie a serious look. "Actually, you should be grateful to Tabitha. It was her who told me that being upset about you was stopping me from concentrating. That's why I came back when I did."

"I was not going to do what those creatures said," Sofie protested, but she shuddered. Then she added, "So, she is talking now, is she? *Magnifique . . .*" She huffed a little grumpy sigh through her nose. "Did she say anything else useful?"

"Only the same thing she said yesterday. That I need to sort things out with my mum."

"Oh, zat! Zat is obvious, I knew zat," Sofie said, sounding very French in her disgust. "But I suppose for a *cat*, zat Tabitha is quite sensible. You should go to Paris and see your mother, Lottie," she said firmly, as though that settled everything.

Lottie stared at her. It was just what Tabitha had said. Everyone seemed to think she would find a way, if only she would try. Lottie sighed. She *was* trying, or at least it really felt like she was.

Sofie flowed into her lap, and snuggled closely against her. Lottie had always gotten the feeling that the little dog was too proud to be cuddled, but now it just seemed the right thing to do. She wrapped her arms around Sofie's sweet, cinnamon-and-chocolate-smelling body, and held her tightly, her cheek resting against the velvet fur.

Then she gasped. A warmth was rushing through her, building to a sparkling heat that seemed to fill her right to her fingertips.

Sofie whined, surprised, and Lottie felt her claws digging into her T-shirt.

"What was that?" she whispered, as the golden fire seeped away from behind her eyes. "What did we do?"

"I think that was your power, Lottie," Sofie said, her voice husky. "I think that maybe we . . ."

"Sofie!" Lottie squeaked joyfully. "It was you! You gave it to me! Does that mean you're my familiar? Please?"

Sofie rested her chin on Lottie's shoulder, and its soft weight fitted. "It seems to be so," she murmured. "We are a pair now, you and I."

They sat together for a few minutes, feeling stunned, just reliving that first amazing moment. Then Sofie wriggled herself around and nudged Lottie in the ribs with her nose.

Lottie grinned at her. "Are you thinking what I'm thinking?"

Sofie's whiskers twitched excitedly. "We *should* test it, don't you think?"

Just then one of the pink mice scampered across the polished floor, searching for chocolate crumbs. Sofie fixed it with a steely glare, and it stopped suddenly, looking panicked. "What? What?" it squeaked worriedly.

Lottie's heart was thumping with excitement and fear — what if it didn't work? What if they'd just imagined it all? Going by instinct, she stretched out a hand toward the mouse, and then lifted her arm slowly upward.

The mouse came too.

"Go on! Go on!" Sofie yapped, bouncing excitedly on the bed. "You're doing it!"

The mouse was four inches off the ground now, trying to run, and looking very annoyed about the whole thing. Its paws were scrabbling air, and it was squeaking furiously. "Put me down! Down! Now! No one asked me if I wanted to be a flying mouse. Put . . . Me . . . Down! Ow!"

That was when Lottie dropped it. It scurried away, pausing at the door, to squeak ear-piercing, mousy curses at them both before sliding down the banister.

"Sorry!" Lottie called after it. She felt a little bit guilty, but mostly she was fizzing inside. She had made a mouse fly! She leaned back against the wall, feeling dazed and happy.

Sofie, being more used to magic, recovered more quickly. She barked sharply in Lottie's ear to get her to listen. "Lottie, I have an idea," she said thoughtfully. "About Paris."

Lottie blinked at her. She'd almost forgotten.

Sofie jumped down from the bed. "Come," she demanded, prancing out the door. Lottie's room was at the top of the house, the only door right at the top of the last flight of stairs. Or so she'd always thought. But now Sofie was sitting smugly in front of a tiny door built in next to the top of the stairs.

"That wasn't there before," Lottie said quietly. She was still feeling rather dizzy.

"It was," Sofie said, "*I* knew it was there. I could smell it. But it does not open. Or at least, I have never *seen* it open."

Lottie looked thoughtfully at the door. She was starting to feel a bit more normal. "But maybe now . . ."

"Exactly!" Sofie nodded, her muzzle stretching excitedly toward the little, quiet, brown door. Uncle Jack had told Lottie that dachshunds were originally bred to go down holes after badgers, which was why they were sausage-shaped. The way Sofie's whiskers were bristling with excitement now, Lottie could imagine her charging down a hole, snapping at a badger's heels.

"What's behind it?" Lottie asked. She was trying to think where the door must go. As far as she could tell, it should lead to the chimney from the kitchen fireplace.

Sofie glanced at her, big black eyes sparkling. "If this is the door I think it is, it is more a question of *where* does it open. . . ." she said temptingly. Then she added, with a sigh, "Of course, we have to open it first."

Lottie looked at the door more closely. "There isn't a handle!" she exclaimed disappointedly. "Do you think we need a key?"

"There is no keyhole either," Sofie pointed out, her head to one side, regarding the door thoughtfully. "I think we should touch it, and see what happens."

Lottie looked at her, suddenly realizing how much more adventurous Sofie seemed to have become in the half hour since their discovery. Previously she'd been far more fond of naps and chocolate than having adventures.

Sofie seemed to see what she meant. She fluttered her thick black eyelashes modestly. "It is the magic," she explained. "I can feel it all over, Lottie. I want to *do* things! Put your hands on the door," she ordered, scrabbling a little, and then standing up with her delicate ginger front paws on the wood.

Lottie laid the palms of her hands on the door. It felt alive, slightly soft and very warm. She pushed gently, but nothing happened.

"You need to pay," a voice purred sweetly.

Lottie and Sofie whirled around, feeling guilty. Tabitha was sitting behind them, her tail wrapped perfectly around her paws.

"What do you mean?" Sofie asked, her voice full of suspicion.

Tabitha's whiskers flickered, and she said nothing.

Sofie glared at her, and then she ducked her head between her paws. "I am sorry," she muttered. "But how do you *know*?"

"I know most of what Ariadne knows," Tabitha

explained. She stood up and rubbed the side of her head affectionately against Lottie's leg. "You and Lottie will find the same thing."

"Pay with what?" Lottie asked. She didn't think Tabitha meant money, and she really hoped it wasn't going to involve blood.

"A hair would do, I think," Tabitha said thoughtfully. "And one of your whiskers, Sofie, if you want to go too."

It was easy enough for Lottie to pull out one of her own hairs, but Sofie refused to let anyone near her whiskers.

"Your fur is too short to pull out," Tabitha said gently. "It has to be a whisker."

"If this doesn't work, I will make your life a misery. . . ." Sofie muttered as she tried to stand on her own whiskers. Lottie wasn't sure which of them she was talking to. Eventually, Sofie managed to get one, though it left her shuddering. "One of my best whiskers," she moaned. "I am lopsided!"

"At last," Tabitha hissed. "Hold them up to the door. Good luck!"

Lottie picked up Sofie, who was still whining, and pressed her hand against the door, holding the whisker and her hair. Then she stooped a little as the door swung gently open — and they were somewhere else.

13

At first Lottie thought it was all a horrible joke, and the door had just led them back downstairs. Then she realized that the voices she could hear were chattering in a language she didn't understand.

"We're here," Sofie said excitedly, wriggling in her arms. "This is Lafitte and Cie, where I was born. Come, let us find Colette." She jumped down and skittered off through the shop, causing a riot of squeaks and growls as the animals in the cages wondered who she was.

Lottie followed her, looking around delightedly. The shop wasn't actually like the shop at home at all, now that she looked carefully. It was light and airy, and the high ceiling was painted with a wonderful forest scene, dotted with birds. It was only when one of the jewel-bright creatures flew past her nose that Lottie realized the birds were real, their perches hanging from the painted walls.

"*D'où êtes-vous venu?*" the bird chirped to her, perching on her shoulder and looking at her inquisitively.

"They want to know where you have come from!" Sofie called back.

Lottie looked at it apologetically, wishing Sofie had taught her more French. "I'm Lottie," she tried to explain. "I came with Sofie, from Grace's, in England."

"Eng-land!" the bird squeaked, and flew off up to the others. Soon they were all chirping, *"Angleterre! Angleterre! Petite fille Anglaise!"* and several more of them flew down to look at her closely. Lottie decided that this Colette that Sofie had mentioned must specialize in birds, like Uncle Jack did with mice.

"Come on, Lottie!" Sofie had trotted back, and was calling her impatiently. Lottie noticed at last that an old lady was watching her from the front of the shop. She had at least three tiny birds perched on each shoulder (it was hard to tell because they kept moving), and she looked rather like a bird herself, her eyes dark and shining and beady.

"Hello, Lott-ee," she said carefully. "So, you bring my little Sofie back to me for a visit, huh?"

Lottie blushed. She realized now that they'd just appeared in the middle of the shop — there was a tiny red door behind a row of cages — and she felt a little rude. "I hope you don't mind," she said shyly.

"Pas du tout, no, no." The old lady waved a hand dismissively, and several birds fluttered into the air, chirping irritably. *"Pardon, mes chéries.* Sofie says you are looking for your mother, yes? Do you have her address?"

Lottie grabbed her mother's last letter out of her pocket and showed it to Colette.

"Ah, that is not far from here! Sofie can show you." And she went into a long discussion in French with Sofie, with lots of arm-waving, and argumentative snapping from Sofie, who clearly thought she knew the way to *anywhere.*

Colette gave them a very smart pink suede collar and leash for Sofie, as she said they ought to *try* to look as though it was Lottie who was in charge of where they were going. Sofie sniffed disgustedly, but she liked the color, and the sparkly crystals on the collar. "French, you see?" she told Lottie. "Never would your uncle sell nice things like this. I look good in pink, yes?"

"Very chic," Lottie assured her, and Sofie rubbed a paw over her nose in embarrassed pleasure.

"Hurry up, Lottie," she said, pulling at the new leash to cover it up. They set off, Sofie trotting ahead along the fashionable shopping street. She got lots of admiring looks, and Lottie could see her preening as ladies cooed over how gorgeous she was. At last she stopped outside a beautiful stone building. "We are here!" she hissed out of the corner of her mouth. "Now what?"

Lottie looked blank. It was clearly quite a nice building, and she could see that the hallway had a man sitting behind a desk, reading a newspaper. She wouldn't be able to slip in unnoticed, and she wasn't quite sure what she was going to say to her mum yet. It suddenly struck her that she needed to explain how she'd gotten here, somehow. *Through a magic door* was not going to work.

Sofie looked up at her and nodded decisively. "We go around the back, huh?" she murmured, and she set off again, scampering down an alleyway at the side of the building. It was full of Dumpsters, and rather smelly, but Sofie darted along, stopping triumphantly by a black metal staircase. "The fire escape!" she panted proudly. "We go up this, and see if we can find your mother's apartment!"

Lottie knew that her mum lived on the sixth floor, so they toiled up the stairs. It was horrible, they creaked, and even though they seemed very solid, the sense of air blowing all around them made Lottie feel as if they were swaying. She wished she could just shut her eyes. Even if she stared at her feet, she could see the ground through the gaps in the metal steps, and it was getting farther and farther away. "Look!" Sofie pointed out excitedly. "Windows, yes?" She was peering nosily into someone's kitchen and Lottie saw with horror that the owner was staring back, and flapping a dish towel at them angrily. They climbed on quickly, but Lottie realized that Sofie was right. If her mum's apartment was by the fire escape, they would be able to see her.

"This has to be the sixth floor!" Lottie panted desperately. "We've been going for ages."

Sofie nodded. "I think so."

Cautiously they peered around the window frame. It was a hot evening, and the window was open. Again, they were looking into a tiny kitchen, but the door was open, and they could see a living room beyond. Lottie's mother was sitting on the sofa, with her back to them.

"That's her!" Lottie gasped.

"Who is she talking to?" Sofie asked, her paws on the windowsill, looking around the kitchen cupboards.

"I'm not sure." Lottie sat down on the step, leaning as close as she could to the window. "I can't see anyone else."

"I think she is crying," Sofie whispered. "She makes the same sniffing noise you do."

Lottie nodded. "She's holding something . . . oh! It's the photo of me and my dad that used to be in our living room at home, I know the frame, that purple one."

Lottie's mum grabbed a tissue from her pocket, blew her nose, and went on talking, very quietly. Lottie and Sofie were leaning right in the window now to hear.

"It feels so unfair, Tom. I have to be here, the company was making layoffs, and I know if I hadn't taken this job, they might have put me on the list too."

Lottie gave Sofie a shocked glance. Mum hadn't told her that!

"But I miss Lottie so much! It was bad enough not

having you, and now I don't even have my baby girl. It's so lonely here, even though the job is exciting, and the people in the office are nice. I can't risk not having a job, and not having enough money to look after Lottie properly, but I just wish I could be at home with her. . . ."

"I don't care about the money," Lottie murmured, her own eyes filling with tears. "I'd rather have her. . . ." She scrambled through the open window, lifting Sofie down after her, and rushed into the living room, forgetting all about not being able to explain how she'd gotten there, and just wanting to give her mum a hug. It felt wonderful, leaning over the back of the sofa, and throwing her arms around her mum's shoulders. It was nearly two weeks since Lottie had seen her, and even then, they'd not been talking. Just smelling her mum's perfume made her feel happy.

"Oh!" Lottie's mum put her hand up, as though to stroke Lottie's cheek, but she didn't turn around. She just sighed, the shuddering sort of sigh that you make when you're getting over a bad fit of crying, and she seemed to relax, her shoulders no longer hunched.

"She can't see us," Sofie said interestedly. "She doesn't know we're here." She was standing in front of Lottie's mum, with her paws on the sofa, looking at her with her head to one side.

"Why?" Lottie cried disappointedly. She wanted to talk to her, tell her it was OK, she could come home.

"I *suppose* because we are here by magic," Sofie said thoughtfully. "Your uncle said that she was unreceptive, no?" She looked at Lottie's mum, still crying quietly, but not gasping like she had been, tears just trickling gently down her cheeks. "She can *feel* you. She is happier, look."

Lottie nodded. It was true. She was too. The weight of unhappiness that had settled in her chest had melted away, now that she knew more of her mum's reasons for going. Tabitha had been right. People did show love in different ways. Her mum couldn't face the idea of not being able to give Lottie all the things she thought she wanted. She walked around to sit next to her mother on the sofa, beckoning for Sofie to jump into her lap. They had a little time. The door would open for them again whenever they went back, and Colette had said she would be up late, and they wouldn't disturb her.

Lottie laid her head on her mum's shoulder, and gazed happily down at the picture she was holding, the glass splashed with tears. Her father's face smiled back at her, sharing their secret, and Lottie felt the sweet sadness of so many might-have-beens. The little Lottie in the photo was smiling, too, but with excitement, and pure happiness as she sat on her daddy's shoulders and clutched his hair. Whenever Lottie had stared at that picture before, she'd been jealous of her other self, who still had a father. This time she felt as though he belonged to her too.

Lottie put out a finger and wiped away the teardrops from the glass. Her mother blinked, dazedly, and Lottie put a hand on hers. "It's all right. . . ." she whispered, leaning over to kiss her. Then she stood up, Sofie in her arms.

They would be back, she was sure. But now it was time to go home.

Join Lottie and Sofie
for a new enchanting adventure!

Where will the magic take them next?

Lottie trailed slowly up the steep lane that led to Netherbridge Hill Elementary School. She threaded her way through the crowd at the gate and slipped into the playground, looking at the school properly for the first time. It was ancient.

Ignoring the little voice telling her just to turn around and walk out of the gate again, Lottie walked very slowly over to the harassed-looking teacher and smiled politely at her. "Hello. I'm Lottie Grace. I'm new. Could you tell me where I should go, please?"

The teacher was nice, at least. She pointed Lottie in the direction of her classroom, told her where the bathrooms were, and said she was looking forward to getting to know her. Lottie felt almost cheerful. It was amazing what one nice person could do to make you feel better. Unfortunately, she then turned around to go to her classroom, and found Zara and her little clique behind her, all smiling sweetly.

"Hello, Mrs. Hartley!" Zara sounded like a model pupil. "Did you have a good summer?"

"Zara! Hello, and hello Ellie and Amy and Bethany. Thank you, yes, it was lovely. Now, girls, you've arrived at just the right time. This is Lottie, and I'm pretty sure . . . yes, she is going to be in Mrs. Laurence's class with all of you. So could you point her in the right direction? Keep an eye on her?"

"Of course we will," Zara promised, looking wide-eyed and angelic at the unknowing teacher. She even put an arm around Lottie and gave her a little hug. "Hi, Lottie! We'll *definitely* keep an eye on her, Mrs. Hartley."

Lottie just bet they would.

Zara was clearly everyone's favorite person at Netherbridge Hill. All the teachers', anyway. Lottie wasn't so sure about the rest of her class. She thought she spotted a few disbelieving looks when Zara gushingly introduced Lottie to Mrs. Laurence. Still, she *was* being very nice. Lottie wasn't sure why. She certainly didn't trust her an inch.

Lottie wished that Zara would just cut the act. It was horrible watching her smile and offer to share her glitter pens so Lottie could decorate her new books. How could anyone actually fake being this nice for so long?

She had to wait all morning, her insides fizzing nervously, as she wondered what Zara's plan was. Then Zara's little group scooped her up with them and headed off to the school hall, which had tables put out in it for lunches. Their fake niceness lasted long enough for them to advise Lottie not to get the shepherd's pie ("Made with real shepherds . . . " Bethany giggled), but then they bagged a table well away from the lunch ladies and the patrolling teachers and trapped Lottie right by the wall, so she'd have to struggle past all of them to get out.

Lottie stared at her plate, waiting for whatever Zara was planning.

"Aren't you hungry, Lottie?" one of the other girls asked sweetly.

Lottie poked miserably with a fork at her baked potato and cheese.

"School food is awful, isn't it?" Zara said sympathetically. "It's got no flavor at all." She reached into her bag and pulled out a small packet. "This should help." She smiled, still looking completely sweet and friendly, and tipped the contents over Lottie's food.

Lottie started sneezing, again and again, her eyes burning. She wondered for half a second if Zara was a witch, too, and had put a spell on her — weird things happening had tended to mean magic over the last few weeks — but it was just pepper.

She looked up at Zara, her eyes running with peppery tears, but she was glad. This she could deal with. She was furious, and it was far better to be angry than frightened and upset by mean whispering. She picked up her plate and tipped it upside down on top of Zara's.

Then she fixed her dark eyes on Zara's round blue ones. Ariadne had taught her how strong the power of a stare could be. It was one of the things that made cats so spooky sometimes.

Zara looked quite disconcerted. Lottie didn't even have to look inside her mind to tell that she'd expected her to collapse in a heap and howl.

"Leave . . . me . . . alone," Lottie snarled, still fixing Zara with her glare, and she pushed her chair back with a shriek that made everyone in the hall turn around in surprise. Then she barged her way past Bethany and Amy, not being particularly careful who she kicked on the way.

The hall was noisy with clattering knives and forks and first-day-of-school chattering, but lots of people were silent as they watched her go. Most of them eyed Zara's table thoughtfully as Lottie headed out of the door.

The teacher on lunch duty intercepted her at the door.

"Are you all right? It's . . . Lottie, isn't it? Do you need anything?" Clearly she'd noticed something was going on, but she wasn't sure what.

Lottie could feel six pairs of eyes burning into her back as Zara and her friends wondered what she'd say. She wasn't going to tell. On her first day, and make herself look like a real baby? No, they'd get away with it this time. At least she'd managed to ruin Zara's lunch too.

Meet the Kreeps

Check out the whole spooky series!

#1: There Goes the Neighborhood

#2: The New Step-Mummy

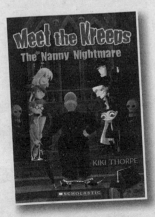

#3: The Nanny Nightmare

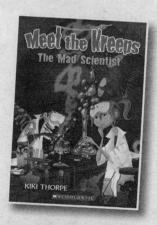

#4: The Mad Scientist

How can one Pet cause so much Trouble?

Runaway Retriever

Loudest Beagle on the Block

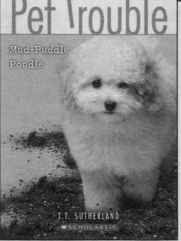

Mud-Puddle Poodle

Read the series and find out!